Renée Harrell

The Atheist's Daughter

Hunting monsters press

The Atheist's Daughter

Hunting Monsters Press

Copyright © by Renée Harrell

Cover illustration by 1 Rat Studio Graphics
contact: 1RatStudio(at)gmail.com

Hunting Monsters Press
www.HuntingMonstersPress.com

This is a work of fiction. The characters and events portrayed in this book are fictional and any resemblance to real people, events or incidents is purely coincidental.

ISBN: 978-0-9829221-4-9

Printed in the United States of America

10 9 8 7 6 5 4 3 2

**This book is dedicated to
Danger, Adventure, and Daring.**

Chapter One

From childhood's hour, I have not been
As others were; I have not seen
As others saw

– Edgar Allan Poe, From Childhood's Hour

From Kristin's Diary

I don't want you to think you've fooled me, Dr. Ron. When Mike, your orderly, your troglodyte in training, brought me this notebook and huge, clumsy pen, I was immediately suspicious. I knew what was up.

I knew you were planning to read everything I wrote. Planned to read the words I'm writing now.

"This is for you," Mike said, thrusting the pad at me. "From the doctor."

"What for?"

"You don't get television privileges for another week," he told me. "Your cell phone's put away. The internet? Forget it. This'll give you something to do. Record your private thoughts and things."

"Like a diary."

"Kind of, I guess." He shrugged, trying to appear innocent, but Mike doesn't do innocent very well. His neck flushed and he looked guilty of something, like he'd stolen money out of my backpack.

"But this is mine," I told him. "My words, my private thoughts, so it's my property. Nobody else gets to read it. Right?"

He smiled at me, then, but he didn't say anything. Lew isn't very bright, he doesn't have a bunch of framed certificates and diplomas on an office wall like you do, but he's learned something you haven't. Picked it up pretty quickly, too.

He's learned not to lie when I'm watching.

I decided to write in this stupid journal, anyway. Lew's right, there's nothing else to do here.

Don't waste your time, thinking you'll discover all of my deepest, darkest secrets. Until today, I didn't have any secrets at all.

Then, when things went weird and I tried to tell people what was happening, what I was seeing, you know what happened.

I got locked up in here.

*

Outside of my room's barred window, the bell in the tower is gonging again. The first time it *BWUNGED!* the orderlies said all of the visitors had to go so Mom left. I'm guessing, since it's dark outside, the *BWUNG!* noise means something new this time. Like, maybe, it's time for lights out.

6

I don't want to turn off the lights. You think I can sleep after everything that happened today?

Seriously?

From inside your basement lair, I'll bet you can't even hear it when the bell gongs. On the surface, in the dormitory where your patients stay, the sound is really loud. It's obnoxious as hell. When the bell sounds, it makes me want to jump out of my skin.

It's enough to drive me craaaaaaazy.

That's a joke, Doc.

You want to hear another joke? You might not think it's funny but it made me laugh.

When they brought me here, dragged me through the gates of Kendall Sanitarium, I totally freaked. I cried, I panicked, and everybody acted like I was this insane person.

Your orderlies circled around me, all of those cold-faced strangers, and I saw you for the first time, standing 'way back from the action. Like, maybe, Psycho Dust might drift from me to you and sprinkle all over your pinstriped suit or your skinny black tie.

I was a mess, I know, but your staff – *you* – acted like I wasn't even human. While I wiped at my nose, trying to keep snot from dripping down my face, Nicole, your short, fat-faced second-in-command, pressed in beside you. She whispered something in your ear.

I heard you say, "Single mothers, Jesus. Take Mama to the Welcome Center and tell her to sit her ass down. I'll get to her in due time."

Nicole nodded, bowing and scraping, practically genuflecting as she backed away from you. So I thought

7

it was hilarious when she showed up outside of my door a couple of hours later.

"Bring the girl," she told pimply Darren, my keeper at the time. "Shit Stain wants to see her."

See, your last name is 'Shinstine' and she acts like you're all big and important when she's at your side but really….

Well, you can probably see why I thought it was funny.

When Nicole leaves, I tell Darren I don't want to go to your office. He says I don't have a choice.

"It's S.O.P.," he tells me. "Standard Operating Procedure."

He escorts me down two flights to your private office. Mom is there, super worried, and you're behind your desk, pretending you care about me. You couldn't care less, I get it, and I even understand it. Every nut in town gets admitted to Kendall, the full can of 'em, so to speak, so what's one more?

But for my mother, this isn't business as usual. She's scared. She can see through your bullshit sympathy act but you don't realize it. You pat her on her hand and don't notice when she slides her fingers back.

Wearing a plastic smile, you start talking about thought disorders and delusions, hallucinations and psychosis. If my blood work hadn't come back clean, you'd have been talking about angel dust and PCP.

Must've been a disappointment, huh?

You don't even look at me until I interrupt your monologue. You finally focus on me when I ask, "Have you ever cheated on your wife?"

"Kristin!" Mom reprimands, her eyes big.

8

You reach for the gold band on your left hand, and you blink a few times, apparently this isn't the part where patients normally speak, this isn't S.O.P., but then you say, "No."

When you speak, I notice your teeth are magazine-white, so perfect, so shiny. I've only seen teeth like those on television. I don't know what you paid your dentist but you got your money's worth.

Then I ask, "Have you ever cheated on your taxes?" and it takes you longer to answer this time. I can almost see your psychiatrist brain whirling, trying to make sense of my questions.

"Never," you tell me.

That's when I hear the sound: *Schhhct!* That's when your mouth vanishes.

When you tell me something that isn't true.

It's just like when Sara Kotch lied about her homework, at school. Exactly the same.

I want to scream when it happens but that's what started this whole thing, right? Instead, I bite my lower lip, like I should have done when Sara Kotch's mouth disappeared.

I pretend your face hasn't gone positively bizarre.

By the way, side note here, I'm going to practice at pretending better. Mom says, practice makes perfect, and I swear to you, give me a few months, I'm going to be the best pretender you've ever met.

This time, still learning how to fake it, I did a good enough job. Mom knows something is wrong, but you're clueless. You pat at her hand. She slides her fingers away for the second time. You start talking about medications

9

and treatment, spouting words like some kind of human textbook, and your face goes back to normal.

I see those square, shiny teeth again. Gleaming at the world.

The first time I saw you, Dr. Ron, I tried to tell you the truth. I called out to you, your goons grabbing my arms, but you turned your back on me. I heard you tell Nicole it was time for lunch. You thought maybe you'd have a nice piece of veal.

Everybody's got their priorities, right?

So maybe Nicole is right and you're a Shit Stain. Maybe you're not. Let me try to connect with you this one last time.

If you ever want to know me, if you really want to help, this is your chance. Treat me like I'm a person, someone needing help, and I'll try whatever you want. Treatments, medications, anything.

Treat me like I'm just another paycheck, Demento #382, and you've lost me already.

I don't think you can cure me but, if you can, I'm ready. I want to warn you, though, I don't think this is my private psychosis. I think this is my secret reality.

When someone lies to me, their face changes. It's scary as hell. If you could see what I see, you'd scream, too.

When their faces change, people turn into monsters....

Chapter Two

Monsters

Cross-legged, she sat upon the concrete floor. A periwinkle linen cloth draped down the sides of the small table in front of her, its violet tassels brushing lightly against her thighs. Miss Sweet shifted her legs, the better to feel the fibers as they caressed her skin.

The pleasure of physical sensation was already fading. Too soon, it would be denied her.

Five years for one, she thought. *It isn't fair. It goes so quickly.*

Too quickly.

Soft footsteps approached her doorway. Turning, she was surprised to see a visitor appear in the opening of her room. A slender woman, middle-aged in appearance and modestly attired, Mrs. Norton stepped through the doorway.

A frown teased at the corners of Miss Sweet's lips. She quickly hid it away.

She should have known Mrs. Norton was coming. That's what psychics do, after all.

They know when bad things are about to happen.

"I want you to throw the bones," Mrs. Norton said.

"Is there a problem?"

"There are always problems. The bones. By morning light."

11

"There's a spotted tom prowling at our back door," Miss Sweet said. "It's ribs show through its matted hair. It's hungry, so hungry it dares lurk in the alley behind our shop. It's even taken a treat from my hand."

"Kill it."

Miss Sweet relaxed.

"To be rid of the beast," Mrs. Norton said, "not for its bones. You know what I want. Not a cat, not a dog. Find a crow. This city is infested with them."

"There's none around here."

"There wouldn't be, would there?"

"Could Mr. Brass help? Or the new one, Mr. Locke?"

"I think not."

"Not to kill the bird," she said hurriedly, "only to help me catch it. To carry the bag and throw it over the crow. It would be my hands on the creature's throat. My reflection in its eye when it died."

"As our young Mr. Locke stumbles after you, setting off car alarms, sending the neighborhood dogs into a panic, what will you tell the police?"

"The police? They don't care about *crows*."

"Might they wonder why Mr. Locke is carrying a cloth sack down an alley way? Or worse, a sack with something wiggling inside of it?"

Miss Sweet fell silent.

She had other ways to see into the future. Tea leaves and gypsy cards rested on the shelf behind her but they couldn't be trusted. There was ambiguity in the patterns of a drowned leaf and the cards delighted in the confusion they caused. Every good scryer knew the gypsy's cards liked to hide their truths.

12

Palmistry was available but not for their kind. She had a crystal ball, years ago, but sold it for pennies, angry at its unwillingness to be directed.

And then there was the seer stone.

The seer stone waited on the table in front of her, lovingly folded inside of a velvet cloth. The stone was true to her but it exacted a price to reveal its secrets. It needed a single drop of human blood, freshly offered and freely given.

Miss Sweet had none to offer. Nor did any of the others.

"Mr. Brass knows how to use his body," she said softly. "He would not be so clumsy as Mr. Locke."

She dared to peek at Mrs. Norton. Was there a flicker of irritation in her eyes, if only for a moment?

If so, it was gone now. Miss Sweet locked her fingers beneath the table, folding her hands to still the tremor in them.

Mrs. Norton said, "Mr. Brass is occupied at the moment. There's a patrol car outside of the building and a Sergeant Foster is at our front counter. It appears the police don't trust Mr. Brass. They suspect he's using our little shop for mundane purposes."

"Drugs."

"Or guns or money laundering. Something trivial." A hint of amusement brightened her face. "Sergeant Foster believes Mr. Brass is a villain."

Well, why wouldn't he think so? *King's Corner Gold and Pawn* leant money to the poor. Respectable society and its guardians always regarded such establishments with suspicion. The shop's owner, then, would be viewed with suspicion as well.

Tall and strong, graying at the temples, Mr. Brass was exactly the kind of man who would own such a business. If *King's Corner* had a villain to observe, it would clearly be him.

Mortal and infinitely careless with the years bestowed upon him, Sergeant Foster would waste hours researching Mr. Brass' background. If he bothered to seek elsewhere, he'd find young Mr. Locke's record was also spotless.

It was unlikely he'd concern himself with the ethereal Alice Poe. Nor would he probe into Miss Sweet's past. So ancient a creature as she must be harmless.

Most shockingly, he'd dismiss the polite and unprepossessing Mrs. Norton out of hand. Not that Mrs. Norton was a villain. Not by his standards.

By his standards, Mrs. Norton was an abomination.

"I hate crows," Miss Sweet said in a whisper.

"Naturally."

Animals hate us, Miss Sweet thought, *but birds are the worst. Crows and ravens are the worst of the worst.*

They scream at us, hoping their cries will awaken the world. If they dared, they'd use their talons and beaks on us.

Only they see us for what we are.

"Tonight," Mrs. Norton said, "as dusk falls. You'll go hunting."

Miss Sweet didn't need her seer stone to visualize the task ahead. Somehow, she'd catch a bird; she dared not fail, even if it took all night. Returning to the pawnshop, the bird shrilling from inside its cloth prison, she'd slam the bag against the floor to stun the miserable

14

beast. Reaching for its throat, looking it in the eye, she'd throttle her enemy.

Once it was dead, things would be better. In her experience, dead was always better.

Her fingers tearing at its feathers, she'd pluck the crow's carcass. She'd boil the meat from its body, letting steam rise into her face as she hovered over the pot. Using a fresh kettle with each change of water, she'd watch the bones roil beneath her until they floated free from their frame. Only then could she collect what she needed.

Five bones. One from each of the crow's wings. One from each of its legs. The biggest one from its chest.

Pulling the linen cloth from the surface of her table, she'd chant her incantation and spill the boiled sticks from her fingers. In her mind's eye, she could see the bones clattering onto the table and bouncing lightly over its lacquered top.

When the bones lay still, they'd provide a tiny window into the future. It wouldn't be much but it would be something. A child's cry, a whispered word, the sight of frost on a window. Some little something.

If she wasn't focused when the bones stopped, if she let herself be distracted, she'd miss the magic when it was offered. If such a thing happened, as it had twice before, she'd have to start over again.

Worse yet, she'd have to tell Mrs. Norton of her mistake. There would be punishment.

She shuddered.

"In the morning, you'll tell me if we can stay," Mrs. Norton said.

"We haven't done anything here. Not yet."

15

"Nor can we, if Sergeant Foster is watching."

"It would be a bother to leave."

"Better to do it now than in the summer."

"Summer." The word slipped lovingly from Miss Sweet's mouth. "When we start to feed."

"Hungry already, love?"

"A little. It's not just me. We all are."

"A young crow," Mrs. Norton said. "One in its prime, with feathers so black they shine. It will tell you what you need to know."

"What if we have to go?"

"I've made some inquiries, just in case. Another business, I think, possibly in Winterhaven. Do you remember Winterhaven?"

Miss Sweet shook her head.

"No surprise," Mrs. Norton said. "It's a little nothing of a town. Still, it's one of my favorites.

"People die so easily there."

16

Chapter Three

From Kristin's Diary

In a few weeks, I'll graduate from high school. The USPS guy just delivered my blue cap and gown in a tear-away envelope. Welcome to the world of biodegradable clothing, guaranteed to dissolve in fifty short years.

Let's hear one last cheer for the Wildcats. Go, Wildcats, go!

Free at last, free at last.

Finally.

One school year and a full-fledged psychotic trauma later than everyone else. Everybody says I'm well-adjusted now, Dr. Ron, just like you promised Mom. Sure, things were tough when I was admitted to Kendall, my two best friends at the time, Jessica and Audrey, never talked to me again, but I got better.

Right?

Of course, I did. I've been cured. The Psych Patrol did its job.

But can I tell you a secret, Doc? Just between you and me and the black-lined pages in this book? The first day home, I quit taking the pills you prescribed. They fuzzed my brain up really badly, they made me feel slow, they made me feel stupid, and they didn't help.

AT ALL.

17

Good thing you explained what the pills were supposed to do. It's easy to know how to act when someone's given you the script.

Every morning, I flush the circular white pill down the toilet bowl. Every night, just before bedtime, I flush the rectangular pink one away, too. It's a waste, sure, but I don't have any choice. I tried to tell Mom I didn't want to take them, didn't really need them, and she freaked. You think *I'm* nuts, you should have seen how she acted.

I caught her once, counting the pills in each of my bottles, just to make sure I was still on my medication. She was mortified when I came up behind her. She pretended she was checking to see if the pharmacy had filled the order correctly.

'Cause the six dollar a month prescription fee starts to add up over a lifetime.

I don't want you to think I'm bitter about our time together. After all, it's not like I wasted eleven months of my childhood behind locked doors, barred windows, and an electrified fence.

Well, no, now that I think about it, it's *exactly* like that. But I did get something positive from the experience.

I started keeping this diary....

Chapter Four

Winterhaven

"Sixty-two, sixty-six," the clerk said.

Kristin's mother nodded, a worried wrinkle creasing her brow. Unsnapping the latch on her wallet, Becky Faraday tugged a credit card from the plastic sleeve holding it.

A year ago, what was it Mom said?

"No more plastic. We'll keep one card for emergencies but that's it. We're done being held hostage by the MasterCard Mafia."

Kristin shook her head. *Just when you thought you were out, they pull you back in.*

She left the store, the door's electronic sensor offering a single beep of protest. The empty sidewalk stretched past her, long and wide, curving at the corner of the mall.

Winterhaven Mall was dying, it was that simple. New, it had boasted of twenty-four stores, a movie theater and a fast-food restaurant. Now, only five shops still survived. Judging by the face of the clothing store's sad-eyed owner, the Mall could expect one more vacancy in the near future.

By Christmas, only the check-cashing store will still be open, she thought. *Not that I care.*

19

In six months, I'll be gone from here, too. When I need to go shopping, it'll be in Ashfork.

Ashfork's three-story Parkway Mall was newer, better, nicer in every way than anything Winterhaven had to offer. In some ways, it was a reflection of the city around it.

Ashfork was growing and expanding, happily embracing progress and all of the promises it offered. Besides its grand shopping Mecca, the city had a thriving Tech Center and a newly-constructed university. Its entire community was thriving, willingly surrendering its farmland to fresh business opportunities and ever-expanding housing developments.

Ashfork was everything Winterhaven was not.

"Mom doesn't care," Kristin told an empty storefront window.

Becky Faraday rejected the very concept of progress. "We'll shop local," she said that morning, "until every last store in our town is closed."

'Shopping local' meant higher prices, fewer selections and outdated styles. Everything was more expensive in their small town.

No Dollar Stores for us. No Midnight Madness or Half-Price Sundays here, no two-for-one coupons.

Live in Winterhaven, you pay full price for everything. You pay and you pay and the stores die, anyway.

"Penny for your thoughts."

Kristin jumped at the sound of her mother's voice. Becky was beside her, the store's electronic buzzer failing to give warning of her exit. Holding a shopping bag in her arms, she looked at her daughter quizzically.

20

"Thinking about finals," Kristin said. With her lie came the sound: *Schhhct!*

A sharp, stabbing noise reverberated inside her head. From experience, she knew only she could hear it. Besides, it was never the sound that bothered her when she lied. It was the physical sensation accompanying it.

The skin on her face started to burn. Her lips pulled together like warm rubber, squeezing against one another. A stab of pain went through her as the lower lip melted into its twin.

The dark glass of an empty shop revealed her reflection. The lower half of her face had disappeared behind a sheath of skin. Smooth and featureless, this barrier of flesh locked her words inside of her.

No one else saw this image. Unless she showed an outward sign of distress, even her mother remained unaware of the transformation. At thirteen, confused by the sudden change in her appearance, the sudden change in her *life*, she'd blurted out everything as it happened to her. Her mouth, the visions, all of it.

Biiiig mistake, she realized now. *First, I got pubes, then I got breasts. How was I to know visions weren't part of the package deal?*

"Comp 202 still giving you a headache?" Becky asked. "No, that was last semester, wasn't it?"

About to speak, Kristin caught herself. The movement pushed her mouth against the flap of skin. Her teeth rubbed the wet surface, scraping its virgin seal.

A drop of blood fell onto her tongue. The dull, metallic taste always made her want to gag.

"Semester before last," she said. The words sounded faint to her, muffled behind their fold.

21

Schhhct! In an instant, the sheath was gone.

Her mouth was back. Cool air pushed in as if it had never left. Darting her tongue forward, she touched it briefly, reassuringly, over each of her lips. Except for the lingering taste of blood, it was as if nothing had happened.

"I thought English Comp was going to be the death of you," Becky said. "Thank goodness for Hawkins."

"My turn now. Poli-sci is Hawk's kryptonite."

"Poor Hawkins."

"Poor Liz."

"Liz? Isn't she going to the University?"

"Only if she manages to graduate," Kristin said. "She's already signed up for summer school. Calculus."

"That's Trevor Silva's subject, isn't it? The teacher who gives three hours of homework for every hour of class?"

"That's the one."

"Liz may never leave high school." Shifting her shopping bag, Becky stepped off the sidewalk.

Following her mother, Kristin stopped abruptly. "Mom?"

Becky waited at the back of their sedan. "I could use some help here."

"Don't you see?"

"What?"

"Piotrowski's Café. The front door is open."

Becky pressed at the car's key fob. "Damned trunk opener. I replaced this battery less than a week ago."

"Somebody cleaned the restaurant's windows," Kristin said. "Somebody painted the wooden shutters."

"Maybe they're finally putting it up for sale."

22

Taking the car keys, Kristin opened the car's trunk. "I think I'll check it out."

"Now?"

"I'll walk home. It's not far."

"It's miles from here."

"I could use the exercise." She started across the parking lot. Taking measured steps, she fought the urge to run.

Please, please, please, Mister Piotrowski. Prove miracles can happen. Open your restaurant again.

Help me escape from Winterhaven.

Chapter Five

Piotrowski's Café remained exactly as she remembered it. Two stories tall, its gingerbread trim and arch-top windows were meant to suggest a whimsical European eatery. While stylish touches decorated the lower level, the second story's charm was diminished by patches of cracked trim and a strip of gray stucco.

Although she didn't remember any of its customers complaining about the café's appearance, Kristin felt the building's need for repair detracted from its appeal. When she shared her thoughts with Martin Piotrowski, he offered his own opinion.

"Customers come here for the am-bi-ance," he said, breaking the word into three pieces, "they're in the wrong city. They want mood-lighting, they can go to Ashfork or Lincoln City. In Lincoln City, all of the swanky places used mood-lighting. People get hungry there, they pay fifty dollars plus tip at some fancy lunch place. The food won't be very good but they'll get a candle on their table."

Martin believed in what he was saying. Opening his business, he sincerely thought good food, good service, and fair prices were all any restaurant needed.

"That and an ad in the Pennysaver," he told her.

Poor deluded Mr. Piotrowski.

He was in front of her now, his thin frame visible through the building's open door. He swept the floor, the broom's bristles pushing at the dirt in short, steady strokes. Climbing onto the front porch, she ran a hand through her hair. She tugged at the bottom of her blouse, smoothing its wrinkles.

Shoulders back, she entered the building. "Mr. Piotrowski?"

His pale blue eyes glided over her before returning to the floor.

"Is there –" Kristin paused, trying to find the right words. "I mean, are you opening your restaurant again?"

The broom stopped moving. Holding its shaft in his large-knuckled hands, he gave her his full attention. "You of all people. You should know."

"Pardon?"

"This isn't a restaurant. It's a café."

"I'm sorry. I mean – I *do* know that."

"Restaurants are for loud and noisy people who don't care what's on their plate. Give them something frozen, stick it in a microwave, they don't even notice. What do they know about quality? They eat biscuits and gravy. They eat those Sloppy Joes."

"Yes." With this single word, she tried to imply that eating Sloppy Joes was the equivalent of shoving your face into a pig trough.

"A café is discrete. A café is for the discerning few. When you worked here, we never had more than eight customers at a time. Did we?"

She shook her head.

"That's why I went out of business!" He laughed. "Eight customers, what was I thinking? I should have served the biscuits and gravy."

25

Leaning his broom against the wall, he opened his arms. Kristin stepped inside them, giving him a hug.

She realized with surprise that she was now taller than the old man. In the months since she'd last seen him, he seemed to have shrunk. She could feel his ribs press against her from beneath his white cotton shirt.

She squeezed her arms around him, her gaze resting on his balding head and its thin wreath of black hair. "I missed you."

He stepped back. "It's been too long."

"I called."

"Message machines, I hate them. Put your finger on the wrong button, you erase everything. Everything!"

"I sent you a card on your birthday."

"A lovely card. It's on the mantel, next to my ceramic pig." Kristin remembered giving him the tiny pink pig when the café opened for business. "You need a job?"

"Me and everybody else. Nobody's hiring."

"Our poor, dried-up little town. In the end, only you and I will still be here. Kristin and Piotrowski's Café. Sloppy Joes, our specialty."

"You might want to ask Mrs. Piotrowski if she approves."

"The missus?" Martin's smile faltered. "She won't care. But...I'll ask her."

Schhhct! His face shifted, blurring as a layer of age-blemished skin melted over his mouth.

Beneath the layer of flesh, his jaw continued to work. "Might be a while, though." His words came to her as if they'd been spoken through linen. "She's in Florida with her sister. All orange groves and sandy beaches."

26

Kristin furrowed her brow in concern. "Where is she, really?"

He regarded her solemnly. Using his shirt sleeve, he dabbed at his eyes. "You always know. Always. How?" His thin chest rose beneath the cotton shirt. "It has nothing to do with her sister. Nothing to do with Florida. She's gone, that's all." His voice broke on the last word.

Schhhct! As if it had never vanished, his mouth was back.

"I don't know where she is," he said. "No phone number, no forwarding address. She doesn't write. She hasn't called. She just left."

"Why?"

"Too many worries," he said. "Things were bad when the café closed. Money problems, sure. Small battles, every day. Never a big fight, never anything important. I'd have done something if it had been important. All of sudden, she wants to leave. *Has* to leave."

Sniffing, he wiped his eyes. "I never could lie to you, could I?"

Kristin remembered short, plump Chandra Piotrowski, her hair as full and white as her husband's fringe was thin and black. Her happy, round face was slow to anger. In memory, at least, she adored her husband.

Kristin could hardly believe she'd left him.

"Nothing to be done about it, I guess." Martin reached for the broom. "Things will work out. Everything always works out."

Not trusting herself to speak, Kristin bobbed her head slightly. She swiveled on her heel, ready to leave.

"The job you wanted?"

27

She hesitated.

Martin twisted the broom handle between his fingers. "If I had one, I'd give it to you. This economy, it's hard on everyone. I just don't have any more money to lose."

"You're putting the building up for sale?"

"For lease, maybe," he said. "A few days ago, I get a phone call from California. Out of nowhere, this lady, this Mrs. Norton, she calls me. She wants to know, would I be interested in renting the building?"

"Are you?"

"Why not? It brings me nothing now."

"How did she hear about the café?"

"I asked her the very thing. A nice voice, Mrs. Norton, pleasant. She said she's visited the Haven a few times and always liked it. Came for the big Pumpkin Festival a couple of years ago and stopped here for a nibble."

"That was just before you hired me."

"So, the service may have suffered but the food was still good. She liked it, anyway. Our place, it always served good food. Our eight customers, they loved us."

"Yes, they did."

"She's talking about a four-year contract, the first year paid in advance. If we agree to terms, she still wants to call it 'Piotrowski's'. Because of the reputation." He practically glowed with pride. "She'll run things with her family. They'll work downstairs, live upstairs. I've told her, anybody decides to use the deep fryer, they're going to smell the grease all night long."

"Think she'll need any help?"

"Depends on how big her family is, I suppose."

28

"Does she seem nice? The lady from California?"

"Nice enough, I guess." His face softened. "Paying a year in advance, it shows she's serious. I wouldn't talk to her if I didn't think she was serious."

Kristin reached out, taking his spotted, dry hand into her own. "Is this okay? Is this what you want?"

"Of course." *Schhhct!* His lips dissolved into one another. "You think I want to open this place again? All the paperwork, the late hours, who needs it? Mrs. Norton can have the café forever as far as I'm concerned."

Chapter Six

Summer

Twisting the doorknob, Kristin entered the house. Following the sound of soft music, she went past the tiled entry and into the living room.

Standing on a plastic drop cloth, Becky wore a paint-streaked purple shirt with the sleeves rolled up and the two top buttons missing. Her blue dungarees were streaked with color at the waistband and showed wear at both knees.

It was her mother's work outfit; her uniform, practically.

So, Mom, what are you going to do when the time comes to replace those clothes? Kristin wondered. *The jeans are interchangeable but the shirt is a one-of-a-kind crime against the fashion world. I know it was Dad's but it's purple and hideous.*

Once it's gone, what will you do for a substitute? Wander from store to store, seeking some outlet barn with a huge inventory of 20th century fashion mistakes – or will you be forced to give up painting altogether?

For now, her mother stood in front of the wooden easel, contentedly working on the canvas in front of her. Passing through the room, Kristin couldn't quite see what she was painting.

Abandoned farm silo, maybe? Weathered windmill? She knew it was something along those lines, anyway. "Famished."

"Fridge," Becky replied.

Kristin padded out of the room, pleased. Too often, her mother got involved in a painting and forgot about food altogether. This time, supper was ready.

Ignoring the dirty pan in the sink, she pulled open the refrigerator door and leaned inside.

"Oh, no."

A big blue bowl sat on the refrigerator's lowest shelf. Dappled beads of water hung from its plastic barrier but didn't obscure the contents inside.

Not mac and cheese. Not again.

This wasn't anything like real macaroni-and-cheese, prepared with actual aged and seasoned dairy goodness. The gummy slop in front of her was colored instead by some powdered plaster-like stuff from a little tear-away envelope. Put the powder into water, stir it around, and drop the mess into a saucepan. When the contents turned an unhealthy Day-Glo orange, it was time to eat.

Cradling the bowl in one arm, she returned to the living room. "Care to explain yourself?"

"Hmmm?"

"Pseudo-food?"

"Uh-huh."

"Not every meal has to come from a box. Sometimes – this is gonna sound wild, I know, but trust me, I saw it in a documentary once – sometimes, people actually prepare fresh food."

"My turn, my choice." Becky brought the tip of her brush to the palette in her hand, its bristles moving from

31

one pool of paint to another. Pushing the pigments together, mixing them into their own shade of pink, she brought the brush up. "Any luck with the job hunt?"

"A promise for an interview. In a month, if business improves."

"That's something."

"It's a kiss-off. I smiled prettily and left the application, anyway." Kristin followed the path of the painter's brush. "You're not working on canvas."

"I wanted to try hardboard this time."

"It's all curves and circles," Kristin said. "That's an awful lot of pink."

"No pink at all, darling. There's cadmium scarlet, yellow ochre, a little lead white. I'm trying for a dusky peach tone." She examined the brush in her fingers. "This beauty is a new hog bristle brush, a Berkeley Number Seven. Special order and not exactly cheap. "

A needle of panic stabbed at Kristin. "How much?"

Becky wrinkled her nose, as if price didn't matter.

"What are you painting, anyway?"

"Something a little bit different. More impressionist than realistic."

"Your rep said everyone loves your landscapes. Your last show completely sold out."

Sixteen paintings, each with a wonderful red dot in its lower right corner, she reflected. *Each dot representing cash in the pocket and another bill paid on time. But Mom knows that.*

You do *know that, don't you?*

"Got a little tired of painting rustic weathered barns. Got a lot tired of painting tranquil country landscapes," Becky said. "Aren't you going to say hello to Susannah?"

Stretched across their worn flower-print sofa, the plump and nearly-naked Susannah Guitierrez wiggled her fingers in a greeting. Wearing only cotton panties, she posed atop a lavender bed sheet. She appeared remarkably comfortable with the rolls of flesh on her sixty-something year old body.

"Hi, sweetness," she said merrily.

Kristin opened her mouth but no words came out. Finding Susannah undressed in her living room was barely more imaginable than opening the linen closet to discover an alligator chewing on the bath towels.

Her mother had painted portraits before, sure, but always on commission, with a check in hand. Those models had always worn clothing while posing.

This was completely different. Two years before, at the community pool, Susannah had covered herself in a modest one-piece bathing suit. A beach towel had hidden her body during the entire outing.

No one in the world will want this painting, Kristin thought. *This isn't art.*

This is abstract pornography.

The doorbell rang, breaking her reverie. Using the opportunity to escape, she said, "I'll get it."

When I was eight years old, Susannah was my babysitter. My babysitter! Artist's model or not, it's wrong to see your babysitter with her breasts hanging out, no matter how many years have passed.

Opening the door, she found Gideon Hawkins in the doorway. Tall and slender, his brown hair was tucked behind his ears with one errant curl dangling down his forehead. Dressed in blue jeans and a loose shirt, he looked like anything but a preacher's son.

33

His father, the Reverend Howard Hawkins, didn't approve of his only child wearing jeans and an untucked shirt when a more respectable suit and tie was readily available in the bedroom closet.

He didn't approve of his son's friendship with Kristin Faraday, either.

"The atheist's daughter?" she'd heard him say once, unhappiness in his voice. As far as she knew, he never said, "The girl they locked away?" or "The one with hallucinations?"

If he cared about such things, he kept them to himself. All he wanted to know was, did Kristin go to church?

She most certainly did not.

Hawkins kept one arm behind his back. When she tried to see what he was hiding, he shuffled sideways.

"Show me."

Solemnly, he brought his arm forward. In his hand, he held a bouquet of flowers.

"Really? I mean, *really?*"

"These aren't for you, Faraday. These are for your mother."

She crossed her arms over her chest. "It won't work, lame ass. She isn't going to be bought for a handful of roadside posies."

"Carnations. Besides, this isn't a bribe. It's a thank-you."

She mock-slammed the door but he slid one foot in front of him. The door bounced weakly against his shoe.

"Jesus," she said.

"Exactly."

He headed for the living room. Her mother held her brush in the air as she considered her work. When he pushed the bouquet toward her, she smiled.

"Carnations," Becky said. "They're lovely."

"Dorothy Parker said flowers were Heaven's masterpiece."

"No such thing as Heaven, young Hawk." Becky shifted to reveal the painting on her easel. "What do you think?"

He puzzled over the curious shapes and colors on the board. A tinge of red crept into his cheeks as he discovered the vaguely carnal nature of her work.

"Well?"

Hawkins cleared his throat. "I, uh – I like your barns."

"This isn't a barn."

"I've noticed."

"Do you like it?"

He shuffled his feet uncomfortably. "It's different."

"Different good," Becky said, "or different bad?"

His attention focused on the painting in front of him, he didn't respond immediately. Kristin knew he hadn't seen Susannah at the other end of the room. Wrapping the lavender bed sheet around her peach-colored body, the older woman walked toward the easel.

"It's not just your barns," Hawkins said to Becky. "I also like your landscapes."

"Thank you." At Becky's words, he released a sigh of relief. She touched his sleeve before he could retreat. "I'm trying something different with this. Something a little less representational. If you have an opinion about it, I'd really like to know."

He leaned toward the painting. "It's mostly curls and circles."

"I think the big circles are supposed to be my breasts," Susannah said from behind him.

Hawkins jerked. Discovering the nearly-nude woman at his back, he crab-stepped away from the easel. His eyes flashed over the thin sheet covering Susannah, finding large patches of bare skin almost everywhere. An expression of horror played across his face.

Susannah studied Becky's work. "I like it."

Hawkins stared at her in amazement. Embarrassed, he dropped his gaze.

Finally, Kristin took pity on him. "The kitchen, Hawk. Let's get some supper."

He quickly followed after her. Placing the bowl in the microwave, she stabbed at its START button.

In a low voice, Hawkins said, "That has to be a sin."

"What?"

"Ms. Guitierrez. What she's wearing. What she *isn't* wearing."

"Count yourself lucky. She was in panties when I got here. Only in panties."

His face wrinkled in contemplation of such a terrifying vision. "Okay, maybe it's not a technical sin, sitting naked in somebody's house. I mean, it's not a covet thing, trust me, and there's definitely no lust issue involved here. But there should be a law."

"What kind of law?"

Speaking in a voice that brooked no argument, he said, "You should have to be much more attractive if someone is going to paint pink swirls and pretend it's your bare body."

36

"Those swirls aren't really pink," Kristin said. "Mom was using cadmium scarlet and yellow ochre."

"What?"

"Plus, a little lead white. Mix 'em together, it turns pink. Pink-ish. Skin tone, anyway."

"Are you trying to make some kind of point here?"

"I'm torturing you with minutiae."

"Why?"

"Punishment," she said. "You brought flowers."

"For your mother." Pointedly, he added, "You'd know if I was lying."

"I see what you're doing. I mean, what you're trying to do."

Hawkins tugged a bar stool from beneath the counter top. Sliding onto it, he looked at Kristin with a guileless expression.

She said, "You're trying to... to – seduce me through my mother."

"Whatever it takes."

The microwave *dinged*. "We've been friends since ninth grade. Can't we leave it at that?"

"One time. That's not so much to ask."

She pulled on oven mitts.

Hawkins asked, "Have you ever done it?"

Holding the bowl, Kristin hip-bumped the microwave door into place. Placing the dish on a metal trivet, she peeled back its cellophane cover. Steam rose into the air.

"Want to know how many times I have?" Hawkins said.

"You've counted?" He nodded. "That's beyond pitiful, Hawkman."

"This Sunday," he said. "You and me."

"I'm busy on Sunday."

"Yeah? Doing what?"

"Doing something else." Reaching into a drawer, she removed a large serving spoon.

"I asked your mom yesterday. She's okay with it. She says it's your decision."

"Thus, the assortment of carnations." She waggled the spoon at him. "Bring all the flowers you want, it isn't going to matter. When the time comes I decide to do it – if such a time should ever come – it won't be because you talked my mother into it."

"Please."

"See, that would have been a better way to start. Too late now."

"Pretty please."

"Forget it." She shoved the spoon into the blue bowl's mouth. "My first time? I'm not doing it this Sunday and I'm certainly not doing it while your father is in the building!"

Opening an upper cabinet, Hawkins pulled out two plates. "Dad wouldn't say anything."

"He'd notice, though. He'd be waiting at the door, wanting to talk to me after."

Hawkins carried the plates to the counter top. "You know what everybody thinks, right? My best friend? Not trying it with me. Not ever."

"I've seen it on TV."

"It's not the same."

"'No' means 'no'," Kristin said firmly. "I'm not going to church with you."

She dug into the bowl, pulling a thick glob of food from its center. Turning her spoon, she let the orange pasta clump fall onto Hawkins' plate.

His face fell. "Mac and cheese? Again?"

Chapter Seven

From Kristin's Diary

Mom's hinting at it, just like last week.

And the week before that.

"You can always go to Hurley," she tells me. "Get your two-year degree." She says this because, despite having a shiny high school diploma in hand, I still haven't found a job.

Find a job? Hell, I can't even get a job interview.

Somehow, life in Winterhaven manages to bump its Suck Score a little higher every day. Whenever I think things have reached bottom, cosmic forces conspire to dig a new, somehow deeper hole.

Mom doesn't get it. Even if I did want to get an advanced degree, it wouldn't be at Hurley. I imagine there are decent junior colleges out there somewhere but not in Winterhaven.

HJC isn't exactly renowned, you know? At least, not in a good way.

The place really only offers three degrees. There's gunsmithing and it's a biggie, drawing students from across the state. Barton Hurley made a fortune in bullets and blood, everybody knows his history, and each semester brings another line of candidates eager to honor the Hurley name.

Not me.

I could go for an Associate Degree in Welding. Which used to offer the potential for a living wage until Hurley International decided to go truly international and moved both of its plants and its smoke-spewing foundry to Tuxtla, Mexico.

Which leaves option #3, a Hurley favorite, the General Degree. As in, "Generally, I don't have any idea of what I'll do with this degree."

If I went to HJC, it would take another two years to get a piece of parchment I don't even want. I've lost enough time in my life. I'm ready to move on.

I wish I could talk to Mom about it. I can't because she'd panic at the thought of her child going to another city. That's what over-protective mothers do. Even if I wanted to discuss my plans with her – something I most definitely do *not* want to do – she wouldn't listen. She'd hate the idea of me leaving. She'd have a thousand reasons why I shouldn't go.

Can't go.

Must *not* go.

So, I'll stay through the summer, doing whatever I can for cash, then pack my suitcases for Ashfork. Once I'm there, I'll find an apartment and get work.

All I want is a barely-there job, where people might glance at the name badge on their server's blouse but can't be bothered to remember it later. A job where nobody notices when the waitress's face freezes and things seem a little wrong.

Then I'll buy a car, nothing fancy but my own wheels, at last, at last....

IF I CAN SOMEHOW GET MORE MONEY.

41

Five hundred and eighty-nine dollars is all I have in the bank and I wouldn't have that much if it wasn't for last year's job at the café. Six bills aren't even enough for a bad set of wheels.

Besides, forget about buying a car, how is a few hundred dollars going to put a roof over my head? In what universe does that amount of money cover first month's rent, last month's rent, and a security deposit?

Ashfork is many things but it isn't cheap. Without a job – a real job, and soon – I'll be on the outside, looking in.

I'll never leave Winterhaven.

No. No. Absolutely not.

Unacceptable.

Chapter Eight

In her bedroom, Kristin's eyes were closed. She was asleep.

Dreaming.

In her dream, she found herself in the center of a lush, green meadow. A lovely cottage sat not far away from her, its charming round windows dotted by perfect droplets of dew. Leading to the cottage was a cobblestone bridge arching over a tiny stream. Past the bridge and its building, there was a densely wooded area. Where the sun peeked through the trees, the ground was nearly golden in color.

It was an idyllic place. Gazing at the scenery around her, she had to admit the setting was marvelous. In all of her life, she'd never been in a more perfect place.

So why does it all feel so wrong?

"Smurfs," she muttered to herself. *Yes!*

Nothing was real here. This was a pretend place, somewhere you'd expect to find fairies or pixies or a colony of little blue Smurfs. They'd sing Smurf songs as they crossed their Smurf bridge, smiling Smurfily as they entered their petite jewel of a cottage. Papa Smurf would lead the parade and Smurfette would be waiting in the doorway.

A black thought intruded: *You don't belong here.*

Where did that come from? she wondered.

43

Pixies and fairies were harmless creatures. Smurfs were just as imaginary and just as sweet. There wasn't any reason to fear them or their ilk.

Nonetheless, the meadow darkened around her, growing less inviting. Although its creator clearly meant for the scene to appear inviting and friendly, it was born out of artifice. Its very existence was as calculated as the numbers in a banker's ledger. Nothing true or honest would be found in this place.

The thought reappeared: *You don't belong here.*

Well, Kristin thought, *where else can I go?*

Beyond the roof of the cottage were the woods. A shadow crouched behind the trees. Avoiding the fingers of sunshine streaking the meadow, the black shade crept from tree to tree, moving closer to the cottage.

Closer to me.

She looked away in fright, felt foolish about it, and forced herself to turn back.

There was nothing there.

For the first time, she felt something wet where the needles of grass nestled between her feet. Wiggling her toes, things felt strangely sticky. She wiped a forefinger against the ground, the grass smearing as she touched it. When she looked at her finger, it carried a stripe of green across its tip.

"What *is* this?" She rubbed her thumb over the stripe of green. The color coated the thumb's pad. She lifted her discolored fingers to her nose.

She liked the odor. She'd lived with it her entire life.

"Linseed oil is why my paints smell the way they do," Becky told her once. "Once the oil evaporates, the paint dries and hardens."

44

There was paint on her finger. Cinnabar Green, to be exact. One of the warmer shades of green, according to her mother.

No wonder things didn't seem real here. They *weren't* real. She was standing in the middle of an imaginary setting.

"It's a landscape," she said. "'Afternoon at Holyford Creek'. One of Mom's paintings!"

The cottage and its rock bridge had never existed in real life. Becky Faraday created it from scratch.

"People love chocolate box art," she said, the day she started painting it, and she'd been proven right. Displayed in the gallery's front window, this particular creation was red-tagged for an eager buyer before her latest show had officially opened.

"It's a dream." Kristin felt her stomach tighten. For the most part, her nights were blissfully empty of memories.

She *hated* dreams.

For the first time, she noticed she was wearing a pair of well-worn jeans and a long-sleeved purple top. Protruding from the shirt's left breast pocket was a black-handled hog bristle paint brush. She pulled it from its pouch.

"A Berkeley Number Seven," Becky's voice said from out of nowhere. "Special order and not exactly cheap."

In front of her was her mother's easel. A rectangle of brown hardboard sat at the easel's center mast.

What was I wearing at the start of the dream? Kristin wondered. *Was the easel here the entire time?*

Why didn't she know?

45

None of this was familiar to her. It was only one more reason to hate dreams: The Dream Master's world played by its own set of rules. The rules weren't fair. Things popped in and out of existence and she had no control over any of it.

She didn't even get to pick where she was. Holyford Creek? It was her mother's worst painting. If she stayed here any longer, she'd get sick from its sugar-sweet artificiality.

"You couldn't stick me in a Davidson print, instead?" she asked the Dream Master.

No answer.

Somehow, she knew she'd never again get an answer to any of the questions in her dreams. She no longer expected one. But one time, years ago, someone *had* responded to her. In her first dream – the first one she remembered, anyway – she was standing barefoot on a beach.

"What are you doing here?" she asked the only other person to be seen, a round-bellied, golden-haired child.

"Playing," the girl told her.

Around them, gray sand was colored with empty cans and bits of debris. The tiny blonde lifted a handful of sand over her head and released it. For a second, the grains formed the image of a seagull before scattering into the wind.

Kristin was only a girl herself, then. "Can I play, too?"

"Uh-huh," said the girl. "Only I get to play."

Suddenly, the stranger reached over and pinched her arm. *Hard.*

46

Crying out, she moved away from this mean creature. "What's your name?" she demanded.

"The Dream Master," the little girl said. Giggling, she vanished.

When Kristin woke up, her arm was bruised.

Still playing with me, aren't you?

She tried to drop the paintbrush but her fist remained resolutely closed. Trying to walk, her feet refused to move. From the waist down, she felt frozen.

Crap.

Atop the easel's fold-out holder was a painter's palette. Feeling compelled to act, she held it as she'd seen her mother do, a thousand times before.

Two fresh circles of paint lay on the palette's melamine surface. The first of the circles was deep red in color. The second oil was stark white and shaped as perfectly as a full moon.

She pushed the brush's bristles into the white paint then carried its color over to the red. Mushing them together, she created a sloppy oblong of fleshy pink paint.

Not knowing why, she slapped her brush against the hardboard. Flecks of paint splashed over her clothing.

She paused, considering what she'd done. She nibbled at the brush's nub.

"I like it," Susannah Guitierrez whispered in her ear.

Shifting her gaze, Kristin didn't see Susannah or anyone else. Taking her brush, she ground it into the pink oblong. Suddenly angry – *Let me wake up!* – she stabbed at the hardboard. Drops of paint flew in the air, spattering her face and neck.

Touching a finger to one of the globules, it felt as wet as water. Its color seeped beneath the tip of her

47

fingernail, staining it. The paint wasn't pink as she expected. Under the white edge of her nail, it was a deep, dark red.

The color of blood.

A rasping noise scraped from the sky overhead. The sound grew, metal grinding over metal, becoming so loud and so harsh she cupped her hands over her ears.

Above her, the sky was flawless except for two cotton-white clouds. The upper atmosphere was every bit as perfect as the rest of Holyford Creek.

Abruptly, the rasping noise ended.

"I like it." This time, the voice came from behind her. Kristin whirled around, finding her mirror-image twin staring back at her.

A lavender bed sheet wrapped around her body, the Kristin-clone smiled. Her teeth were uneven and yellowed from too many years of smoking.

It was the mouth of an older woman. It was Susannah's mouth.

"I like it," the clone repeated, each word spoken in her neighbor's voice.

Kristin caught her breath. Ignoring her twin, she focused on the painting. The rectangle of hardwood had lost the splashes of pink she'd pressed upon it. It waited in front of her, so shiny and white she almost expected to see her reflection in it.

From somewhere in the Cerulean Blue sky, metal ground against metal again. Trying to ignore the building noise, she reached out to touch her painting.

Offering almost no resistance, the hardwood surface folded under the pressure of her fingers. It didn't feel like painted wood at all.

It felt like – plastic.

Something's wrong here, she thought. *Something's very, very wrong.*

Overhead, the sky shrieked down at her.

* * *

"What is it, honey?"

Kristin awoke to find her mother leaning over her bed.

Concerned, Becky said, "You were calling out in your sleep."

"Bad dream."

"Monsters? The boogeyman?"

"I'm a few years past the boogeyman, Mom."

"Sorry."

"There was this awful noise," Kristin said. "It kept coming and going. Screeching at me. Then – then I touched some... plastic."

"Plastic." Becky straightened up. "Ahhh." The worry lines on her forehead smoothed away. "It's past my bedtime."

"But...."

"Long day tomorrow." She hit the bedroom light switch and the room returned to darkness. "G'night."

She closed the door softly behind her.

Kristin kicked at the bed sheet on top of her, shoving it off of the bed. It was lime-green in color, not lavender, but she didn't want the fabric anywhere near her. Folding upon itself, the sheet crumpled to the floor.

Her mother didn't understand. How could she? Kristin wasn't sure she understood, either.

49

The noise in the dream was unpleasant, yeah, but when she'd thought to cover her ears, it lost its power. The sound hadn't frightened her.

What *had* scared her was the painter's board sitting upon her mother's easel. In dream world logic, its surface transformed into plastic when she wasn't watching. During its change, the board gained a chemical smell so strong it made her want to gag. Her heart raced when she stretched out a trembling hand to touch its face.

When her fingers pressed the cool, unmarked surface – something inside of it pressed *back*.

What did it mean, anyway? She didn't know. She only knew that, most times, her dreams came true.

This wasn't the way the things were supposed to work. She'd read enough books, seen enough television, to know what dreams were like for other people. For them, dreams were pleasant, nightmares were scary, and neither was real.

For that matter, she knew what the world was like for other people. No one ever spoke of seeing a liar's face melt. No one complained about their own lips fusing together.

She punched at the pillow beneath her head.

What's wrong with me? Why can't I be like everyone else?

Why am I such a freak?

Chapter Nine

Birth of a Freak

His hand tightened around the hammer's grip. "What do you want?"

Standing nearly a foot shorter than the muscular man, the pretty woman brushed a strand of brown hair from her green eyes. "You heard me."

The man's powerful shoulders shifted beneath his stained and dirty t-shirt. He frowned, the curve of his lips bringing a hint of menace to his pleasantly-attractive face.

"The sink needs some attention," Becky Faraday said. "Today, not tomorrow. It's leaking."

"Becks," the man said, the low growl of his voice softening, "I'm tired. I've spent the whole day working on the bookshelf."

"You did a good job." Lifting up on her toes, she wrapped an arm around her husband's neck. She kissed him warmly on the lips. "Fix the faucet."

Rick Faraday lowered his hammer to his side. "This is supposed to be my day off, you know."

"Lucky man. You get to spend it with me, instead."

"Fixing up our fixer-upper."

"What could be more fun?"

"I could think of a few thousand things," he said. "Besides, we're out of plumber's putty."

"The hardware store will have more."

51

Wearily, he leaned against a sawhorse. Reaching out, he caught his wife at the waist and pulled her onto his lap. "Remind me why we bought this dump."

Curling one ankle over the other, Becky relaxed against his chest. "It was all we could afford, my dear. Besides, we like it here. Great neighborhood, close to work."

"You need to quit your job. Seriously. You don't belong in a bank. You're an artist."

"It's near to your job, too." She ran her hand through his close-cropped hair. "Plus, the neighborhood is decent and Grove Elementary is only two blocks away. Once she's old enough, Kristin can walk to school."

"She'll need to learn how to crawl first."

"By then, maybe the kitchen sink will be fixed." Standing, she tugged on his arm. "Up and at 'em, Mister Faraday. There's work to be done."

Straightening, Rick said, "Did you hear that? The scraping noise?"

"It came from the baby's room." Becky's eyes widened. "Kristin!"

Moving past her husband, she started to run. Rick said, "It's only a noise, hon."

Feeling foolish, he followed her.

Entering Kristin's bedroom, with its paintings of pink hot air balloons drifting across aqua-colored walls, he knew instinctively that Becky had overreacted. Normally level-headed, she turned into an Amazon Warrior when she thought their daughter was threatened.

He remembered what had happened the week before, when a bee had foolishly dared to buzz from beneath the bonnet of Kristin's stroller.

52

Careless little bee, he thought. *Very squished, totally obliterated, hapless little bee.*

Becky sobbed, the noise dying in a choking sound, strangled inside her throat. Her body sagged and he slipped his arms around her for support.

Kristin's crib was empty. Above it, the wire-mesh screen was gone from the bedroom window.

Grabbing at the crib's top rail, his wife composed herself. "Find our baby," she said, in a voice so flat and serious he knew he'd never forget it. "I'll call the police."

Clutching the window sill, he leapt through its opening. Rose bushes grabbed at his legs as Rick fell to the ground. Staggering to his feet, he shaded his eyes from the bright light above him.

On the sidewalk far ahead, a slight figure went briskly down the pavement. Despite the warm day and its cloudless sky, the figure wore a brown suede overcoat with its hood up. The walker's arms were crooked, as if they were holding something.

Rick sprinted forward.

It's a woman, he decided, *it has to be a woman, so small and slim. I can catch her, thank God for all of those 5K's.*

Of course, I can catch her. She isn't even running.

The street was empty. The woman passed the only car in sight, a neighbor's green Pontiac, without slowing at all.

What if she's one of the neighbors?

It was a staggering thought. Six months ago, they'd moved to Winterhaven and found an apartment. After a brief house hunt, they were new, still, to this area. They hadn't met many of the people on their block.

Was this woman watching when they moved in, her fevered eyes focused on Kristin's bassinet? Did she have an accomplice, a boyfriend or a husband, even now peering out from behind closed curtains?

What if the accomplice had a weapon? Worse, what if this woman carried a gun or a knife in one of the overcoat's large, rectangular pockets? Would she hurt Kristin?

She could try. He wouldn't let it happen.

Still too far away for him to stop her, he saw her lower a bundle to the sidewalk. A tiny arm emerged from the baby blanket, displaying little fingers curled around an infant thumb.

Dear God, he prayed. *Dear Jesus. Please protect my little girl.*

I'll do anything, I'll give you anything, but protect her, protect her, no matter what, protect her!

His heart, already pounding, seemed as if it was about to come out of his chest. "Don't!" he cried.

Don't – what?

He didn't know.

Just... just... don't....

Behind him, the front door of his house banged open. Becky called out his name as she came down the steps.

The hooded figure didn't give any indication she'd heard either of them. She squatted over Kristin, her hands holding the baby's torso as she raised the infant. Before Rick could stop her, she pushed a pink tongue from between her thin lips and licked the side of the baby's face.

54

"What the hell are you doing?" He heard the rage in his voice as he reached the kidnapper but a tremble underscored his words.

He grabbed Kristin from the crazy woman. She released the child easily, almost as if she was returning her.

Kristin's lovely brown eyes studied him curiously. She appeared unharmed except for her cheek. Where the woman's tongue had touched her, the skin glowed an angry red.

Panting, Becky raced to his side. "Is Kristin okay?"

Circles of sweat and terror staining the underarms of her shirt, she took the baby in her arms. She covered Kristin with the polyester blanket, as if the wrapping might provide another layer of safety for their child.

"You –" Words failed him. Rick told the stranger, "You don't go anywhere."

She studied him, her expression strangely unconcerned.

Uh-oh. He'd read about women like this. In the tabloids, they were labeled *S.O.S.*: *Single, Obsessed and Scary.*

Lonely and desperate, the S.O.S. would do anything for a child to call their own. They weren't truly evil, no, but they were definitely insane. Insane to think about stealing another family's child. Insane to think they could get away with such a terrible crime.

Becky barely glanced at her child's abductor. As she cradled Kristin in her arms, he saw the red glow was gone from the baby's cheek.

"Go inside," he told his wife. "Call the police again. Tell them we've caught the kidnapper."

She shook her head. The baby in her arms, she half-ran down the sidewalk and into their house.

The hooded woman watched her go. Although she made no effort to leave, he grabbed at the stranger's jacketed arm. "You're staying here."

At his touch, the overcoat fell free from the woman. Its limp sleeve captured in his fingers, the jacket floated forward effortlessly as if her body had only provided a framework of minimal support.

For a moment, he imagined the overcoat had pulled *through* her. He shook the sleeve, letting the garment spill to the sidewalk.

Middle-aged, with curly, brown hair cut just above her shoulders, the woman remained in front of him. Wearing a tan top with matching trousers, she didn't appear unbalanced. She looked....

Normal.

She said, "I wasn't intending to leave. Not yet."

Unperturbed by Rick's anger, she didn't sound afraid. She didn't even seem concerned.

"You're sick. You need help."

"Please." She acted offended, as if such name-calling was inappropriate.

"You can't take someone else's baby," Rick said.

"I gave her back, didn't I? I had no interest in keeping the whelp. Heavens, no." The woman acted surprised Rick would even consider such an idea.

"I only wanted –" Her tongue flicked out from her mouth, wetting her lips, "– a little taste."

"What's wrong with you?" Rick twisted his head, hoping someone was coming to help.

Sirens should have been wailing.

It's a federal crime when someone is abducted, isn't it? Especially a child?

Why aren't police cars racing toward us, tires squealing?

There wasn't a patrol car to be seen. Instead, a UPS driver left a package at a corner house before climbing into his vehicle.

Rick saw Becky waiting on the porch deck. His wife gave a short nod, telling him she'd called for help. He gestured with his head, wanting her safely inside, and she seemed relieved. She returned to the house, the door closing behind her.

The UPS van rumbled closer to them. Over its engine, Rick heard the first, faint sounds of an approaching siren.

It's taken long enough. He smiled.

The woman smiled back at him. Reaching out with a thin arm, she tugged at his sweat-stained shirt, drawing him closer. When she did, her lips opened and her jaws stretched impossibly wide.

Inside the maw of her mouth, Rick saw a blur at the back of her throat.

What the hell? Is there something moving *in there?*

As if reading his thoughts, the woman snapped her jaws shut. Her mouth returned to normal as he tried to escape. He struggled against her grip but she held him effortlessly, as if he had no more weight than the infant she'd snatched.

"Oh, no," he said.

"I need one more thing from you, love, if you don't mind," the woman told him.

He stared at her.

"I need you to die."

Rick felt her free hand grip the leather belt at his waist. She lifted him from the ground as he tried to scream. The sound caught in his throat.

This can't be happening.

It was so absurd, this middle-aged woman raising him skyward. It was impossible. It was some type of bizarre hallucination.

It isn't real. It can't *be real.*

She threw him into the street. Flailing through the air, he got a glimpse of the UPS driver as he slammed on the brakes. The truck hit him squarely across the body, sending him into the air.

He felt the impact when he struck the ground, his arm twisting awkwardly behind him. He heard his bones snap. Somehow, he didn't feel any pain. He coughed once and his mouth filled with blood.

The blue sky swam above him. Faintly, as if from some distant location, he heard the van driver cry out in alarm. He tried to find him but he couldn't. His neck didn't work any longer.

The only person he could see was the crazy lady. She stood over him, her skin suddenly as colorless as a ghost in an old black and white movie. Like a ghost in one of those movies, he could see through her.

Behind her, there was a white Elm tree. Its oblong green leaves were beautiful. Funny he hadn't noticed it before.

The woman's mouth stretched wide as she inhaled. Shimmering waves rolled off of him, bent rays of refracted light sucking his breath away. She arched her back in pleasure and gave a soft moan. It was an unearthly sound.

Rick felt himself growing weaker. Fading, he watched as the translucent woman grew in substance. Color flooded her empty shell as his own body grew cold. With the loss of warmth, he felt like he was the one who was becoming a ghost.

Until, at last, he didn't feel anything at all.

Chapter Ten

When Hawkins called, saying they needed to talk, Kristin was lost.

Talk about what?

He picked her up in his ratty, black Hyundai – washed and vacuumed for a change but, somehow, still smelling faintly of last weekend's fast-food burritos – and they drove in silence toward the center of town.

She was surprised to see him pull into a far corner of the Winterhaven Mall. "You really know how to show a girl a good time."

Hawkins unsnapped his seat belt and faced her. His dark eyes were solemn.

Oh, no, she thought, a sinking feeling settling upon her. *Not the Serious Face, Hawk.*

Serious Face is never good news.

He'd shown her his Serious Face when his father was going to take a parish job over in Baltimore – and then reverted to Goofy Face the second his father changed his mind.

He'd given her Serious Face when Sheri Edmiston broke up with him and he thought his life was over. Serious Face lingered until two weeks later, when he met Michelle Persbrandt.

He'd even pulled out Serious Face when she failed to place in the Tri-State Debate Competition. Once he

60

realized she didn't care then he didn't care, either. Serious Face had remained banished... until now.

"What is it?"

He took both of her hands in his.

What's going on? she wondered. *Do you have a terrible disease? Or did you bowl a 120? Is the world ending or did you find a pimple on your ass?*

Honest to God, Hawkins, you need to set some boundaries on Serious Face. If you're going to use it, save it for something really important.

Please *don't let this be anything really important.*

"There's something I need to tell you," he said.

"Okay."

He didn't speak, as if he didn't know what to say. Outside, a car's engine growled.

Kristin's eyes flicked over to the rear-view mirror. A candy apple red Dodge Challenger was reflected in the glass, speeding across the parking lot and in their direction. "Hawkins."

"I'm trying to think, okay? Let me find the words."

The Challenger's polished body glistened under the sun as it drew closer. The nose of the car swerved and the vehicle raced toward them.

"Hawk!"

The roar of a V8 engine filled the air. Hawkins twisted around as the car filled the window behind them. Its horn blared, frighteningly loud, and, instinctively, Kristin and Hawkins clutched at one another.

At the last second, the car darted to its right. With a shake of her long, red hair, the driver sped past them, laughing.

61

Hawkins shoved at the driver's side door. It creaked open and he spilled into the parking lot. Climbing to his feet, he raised a finger to the sky. "Eff you, Liz!"

In response, the car's driver blared the horn even longer. Her car bumped out of the parking lot and onto the street encircling the mall.

He leaned against the car's hood. Sliding out of the passenger seat, Kristin joined him.

"Liz Wheeler is such an idiot," Hawkins said. "Always looking for excitement. Going a little too fast, cutting things a little too close. Grandma's spoiled little brat."

"A little spoiled. 'Eff you'? You said that?"

He shrugged.

"An 'f' is a letter," Kristin said. "Not a verb. Not a noun."

"She could have hit us. It pissed me off."

"See? That's the way people talk. They say, 'piss', they say, 'crap' —"

He raised a hand to interrupt her. "I know the words." A little defensively, he added, "I'm trying not to say them."

"Since when?"

"Since yesterday." Serious Face returned. "I applied to Oklahoma Trinity."

Kristin's heart sank.

"Dad's a big supporter of the school. For years, even before I was born. They're going to take me. I mean, I don't *know* it but I know it. It's practically a given."

"Oklahoma Trinity."

"The seminary."

62

"I know it's a seminary. You father dropped its color brochure in my lap, remember? He made sure I went to the website, too. Sprawling campus, student dorms, administrative offices, all conveniently grouped in one enormous location."

"It covers, like, six city blocks."

"Big isn't everything."

Hawkins said, "It's in Oklahoma City."

"Of course it is." Kristin heard the flat, bitter tone in her voice. "No better place for a would-be preacher than Jesus Central." She squeezed her hands into fists, trying to hold off her rising anger.

"It's not Jesus Central. It's an okay place. It's pretty decent, actually. I've been there."

"It's miles and miles from here. Forever from here."

"Tell me you're okay with this. Okay with my decision."

But she wasn't okay with it.

How could he go and leave her here? He couldn't wait a few more months, give her an opportunity to raise some money, and move to Ashfork, instead?

Guess not, she thought.

To hell with Oklahoma City. To hell with you, Gideon Hawkins.

"Kristin?"

You don't get it, do you? she asked him silently. *Naturally not. You're a guy.*

You think I should give you a hug. Force a smile. If I pretend I'm happy, we can have the summer together. Nothing more than that but, for now, at least, the summer.

63

All I have to do is fake it. Like I've done a thousand times before.

Knowing how to respond, she didn't act. She was still too mad.

"I've got to do something," he said. "Go somewhere. Oklahoma Trinity might not be the perfect choice but what if it is? You ever think of that?"

She had thought about it. How could she not? The Reverend hadn't exactly been subtle in the hints he'd dropped. But Hawkins had always dismissed his father's suggestions with a laugh. He hadn't seemed remotely serious about the Christian college.

Until now.

His face clouded. "Every time I try to talk to you about something important, you shut down. The silent treatment really gets old sometimes."

Bending down, he quickly tightened the laces on his shoes. "Screw it."

Stiff-legged, he walked off.

Go then, Kristin thought. *You think I care? Why the hell should I care about you when you don't....*

WHY DOES THIS HURT SO MUCH?

Kristin hurried to join him. Hawkins' neck was rigid and his jaw was set.

She guessed it was his turn to try the silent treatment. "I don't think you're allowed to say those kinds of things."

His head faced determinedly forward.

"At seminary, I mean."

Nothing from him.

64

In the past, he'd frequently complained about her periods of silence. At least she knew her reasons for keeping quiet.

Hawkins, on the other hand, was just being stubborn.

"Would Moses have used that kind of language?" she asked. "Do you think he ever went, 'I've got sand in my tightie-whities, screw it, I'm going home'? Would Daniel have said, 'What do you mean, lions? Screw it, I'm hitting the spa'?"

The muscles in Hawkins' mouth worked to keep him from smiling. "The spa?"

"Nebuchadnezzar's Tanning Salon and Spa. Big, big chain. Huge in Oklahoma."

He stopped, facing her. "Are we okay?"

"Always."

"You have to tell me I can go to Oklahoma City. I want to hear you're good with it."

She forced a smile. It felt as plastic as a Halloween mask. "I'm going to miss you."

"Not exactly the same thing."

"As good as you're going to get for now." She blinked back tears. "I'd take what I was offered if I were you."

"Deal."

They stood together awkwardly. Finally, Kristin shrugged. In response, Hawkins raised an eyebrow.

They started walking again.

He said, "School starts in September."

"That bites."

"I'll text, I'll call. I'll e-mail."

"You don't even have a cell phone."

"I'll get one, I promise. Something shatterproof, this time. You won't even know I'm gone."

She felt like he was gone already. "Seminary or not, those text messages better not get all religious-y on me. I don't want to read any 'Honor thy' or 'Thou Shalt Not' stuff."

"Then you don't send me any political bull or celebrity gossip."

"You like gossip."

"Maybe I do, maybe I don't." Stopping abruptly, he stared across the road. "You see that?"

A moving van was parked in front of Piotrowski's Café. The rear roll-up door was up, exposing a cargo hold full of cartons and a metal rack extending over the sidewalk.

Martin Piotrowski walked down the ramp, a box in his arms. At the end of the ramp, a woman waited for him. She wore a dress in a gold leaf print with a sequined belt cinched at her waist. Her frame was small and her arms were bare.

It can't be. Kristin clutched at Hawkins' arm. *I can see through this woman.*

Literally, right through *her.*

She couldn't see past the dress or through the bracelet, but wherever there was skin, the woman was translucent. Without flesh, organs or bone, she presented the outline of a person, a glass woman. If it hadn't been for the fabric she wore, she'd have been nearly invisible.

A tall man stepped out onto the ramp, carrying a large cardboard container. His long sleeve blue shirt was rolled up to the elbows and open at the collar. Like the woman in yellow, his form lacked substance.

66

Gazing into his face was like gazing through a crystal globe, the images behind him visible through his skin and only slightly distorted by being seen in such a manner.

Like the woman, he was a ghost.

"What's wrong with those people?" Hawkins said.

Chapter Eleven

Kristin squeezed Hawkins' arm tightly. "You see it, too?"

"Of course, I do." He reached for her fingers, softening the grip on his arm. "That's not right. Old man Piotrowski, working in this heat? He'll have a stroke."

Hearing Hawkins' words, the woman turned from Martin Piotrowski and looked directly at them. She narrowed her eyes and, for a moment, it seemed to Kristin as if she was surprised.

Surprised and frightened.

Martin carried his box into the restaurant. The tall man followed after him but was stopped at the doorway by the woman in the gold leaf dress.

"Mr. Locke," she said, the words floating to Kristin as if carried on a current of air. The woman dropped her voice.

Mr. Locke nodded. Lowering his container to the ground, crystal muscles bunching under the thin fabric of the blue shirt, he slapped his hands together, as if to brush the dirt from them.

He gazed across the black asphalt, the irises of his eyes hanging like dark half-marbles in the empty sphere of his face. It was beyond creepy. Although it was hard for Kristin to see the finer details in his expression, she could have sworn he was smirking.

Not bothering to check for traffic, he lurched toward them, his stride smoothing as he crossed the street. "Hey! What do you think you're looking at?"

"Oh, boy," Hawkins said softly.

A slender man with delicate features, Mr. Locke's arms were lean but muscular and his shoulders were wide. Still appearing as if he'd been carved from glass, he didn't seem nearly so ephemeral when he was standing in front of them.

He said, "Alice Poe doesn't like how you're staring at us."

The thin woman, Alice Poe, remained at the side of the moving van. Glowering, Hawkins opened his mouth to speak. Kristin put a warning finger against his lips and the motion surprised him. His mouth snapped shut.

"The two of you seem a little slow so maybe you didn't understand me the first time," the glass man said, a threat rumbling beneath his words. "I'll ask one more time. What are you looking at?"

"Nothing," Kristin said honestly.

The answer amused him. "I could say the same, young meat." He tipped his head toward Hawkins. "What's this? Bring me a present?"

Crossing his arms, Hawkins stepped in front of her. *Protecting me,* Kristin thought. *But from what?*

"The boy doesn't know, does he?" the glass man said. "You didn't tell him. I'll bet you wouldn't even know *what* to tell him."

Hawkins turned toward her. When he did, Mr. Locke frowned. Pinching the younger man's chin between his fingers and a thumb, he forced him to face forward.

69

An expression of pain and fear filled Hawkins' eyes. As empty as he appeared, Mr. Locke was apparently quite powerful. A pleased smile lifted his lips as he scanned up and down the younger man's body. "Nice."

Hawkins shrank back. Snorting derisively, the glass man returned to the middle of the street. He stopped, holding an empty hand out to an approaching car.

"Glad you know to keep your secrets, little girl," he called to Kristin. "Now go bother someone else. I have work to do."

"What if I don't?" Kristin called after him. Striding toward the moving van, he didn't answer.

"What was that about?" Hawkins asked her. "What secrets?"

She didn't know what to say.

"What's going on?"

"Piotrowski's Café is in business again," she said. It offered enough truth to let her keep her mouth. "Martin leased out the place. New management. New employees."

"You're not thinking of applying for a job, are you?"

"No."

"Good. Because that guy creeps me the hell out." Hawkins rubbed at his chin as if to wipe away the memory of the stranger's touch. "Did you see how he looked at me?"

Mr. Locke stepped around the metal ramp. Carrying the cardboard container, he brought it into the restaurant. Alice Poe followed behind him.

Before the café's door could close, Hawkins threw a hand up into the air. "Eff you!"

Kristin grabbed at his arm. "Let's go home."

Chapter Twelve

Mrs. Norton led Martin Piotrowski to the café's front door. "Thank you for all of your help," she said. "You're a darling."

"There's still a lot to do. Most of the boxes haven't even been opened."

"We'll manage."

"You're sure?"

"I am." She patted the side of his face. "Your eyes aren't very good at night, you've said so yourself. It's getting late and I wouldn't want you to have an accident on the way home. I might have a need for you later."

Reaching for the coat rack, Martin plucked a gray felt hat from its upper rack. Nestling the hat upon his balding head, he dipped its front brim toward Mrs. Norton and left.

She closed door behind him, locking it. Mr. Locke entered the dining area with Alice Poe at his back, following nervously.

Mr. Locke said, "Why do you waste your time with that fossil?"

Opening a thin, rectangular box, Mrs. Norton tore off its end tab and reached inside. Stepping into the café's picture window, she positioned a UNDER NEW MANAGEMENT sign in its lower left corner.

"He wants you," Mr. Locke said. "You can smell the lust on him."

"Watch your tongue," Alice Poe told Mr. Locke. He scowled at her and she shifted uneasily.

"He's old meat," Mr. Locke said. "Since when is old meat worth the bother?"

Mrs. Norton tugged for the string controlling the window's vertical blinds. The white slats slid, sheet-like, to the base of the window. With a twist of a plastic rod, she closed them.

Only then did she focus on Mr. Locke. "You're still new to our family. Are you already unhappy with how I do things?"

"I didn't say that."

No, he hadn't, but from the way he acted, she knew differently.

It's going to be a struggle with this one, she thought. *Still learning to crawl, he wonders why he isn't allowed to run. Worse, he thinks he has power.*

Power? Him?

His strength is only great in comparison to those we feed upon.

She decided to allow his subtle display of rebellion. This time. After all, he was hungry. It was a new sensation for him, this hunger, and not everyone handled it well. Once he was filled, his color and features returning to him, she would reassess his potential.

Alice Poe saw the shell and could barely wait for its embodiment. Enfleshed, Mr. Locke would be full-lipped with prominent cheekbones; tightly-muscled but still masculine. He'd be pretty for a male and Alice Poe liked them pretty.

A vapid, shallow little thing, Alice Poe had bitter lessons ahead of her but she knew enough to do as she was told.

"It's loneliness you smell," Mrs. Norton said. "Martin's wife left him and his best friend died a few months ago. He feels he no longer has anyone who cares about his well-being. He barely cares about it himself."

With those words, Mr. Locke's expression changed. It was very near to lust itself.

Pity he'd never shown as much interest in Alice Poe.

"He has no one?"

"Miss Sweet will do his reading soon enough. He's quite excited at the prospect. He tells me he's never visited a 'psychic' before. We'll see what's in store for Martin. Perhaps he'll surprise us."

Mr. Locke's tongue licked greedily at his lips.

Entering from the hallway, Mr. Brass drew a brown rag over his crystalline hands. "It's done."

"I hadn't expected it to take so long."

"Me, either." His broad features grew pinched. "Things take longer when you have to do them by yourself."

Mr. Locke said, "I had my own work to do."

"And I'll bet Alice Poe did most of it."

Mrs. Norton raised a finger and Mr. Brass fell silent. "Tell me about the fence."

"It's solid enough." He dropped the rag onto one of the circular tables dotting the dining room. "Eight-foot tall, it runs both sides of the building and across the back. Nobody's going to see into the yard. I ran a heavy chain through the gate, put a padlock on it. The most expensive model in the hardware store."

"Good."

"What we need is some cut wire for the top of the fence. It slices skin like a razor blade. Nobody climbs over a fence with cut wire on it."

"I don't think so."

"We used it in Lancaster. In Bedford, too."

"Yes, we did. It's appropriate for an auto shop or a junkyard; I suppose it's almost expected. It's out of place for a small-town café."

"We were glad to have it in Bedford."

"This is Winterhaven. Here, the citizens feel they can trust one another. They show their trust in little ways. They help their neighbors. They watch one another's homes. Sometimes, they even leave their doors unlocked." She allowed a tiny smile to tease her mouth.

Mr. Brass and Mr. Locke grinned broadly, as if they could barely believe their good fortune. Only Alice Poe remained subdued.

"Did you see her?" she asked, in a voice so small Mrs. Norton barely heard it. "The Other?"

Mr. Locke said, "Don't worry about her. She almost pissed herself when she saw me."

"Is she one of yours?" Alice Poe asked Mrs. Norton.

"I imagine so."

"She won't come back," Mr. Locke insisted. "Why would she? She doesn't know what we are. She doesn't even know what she is." Alice Poe reached for the reassurance of his hand but he denied her, curling his fingers into a fist.

"You're scared of a girl? One of their kind?" Mr. Brass shook his large, square head disbelievingly. "She's nothing."

74

"You didn't see her. I did. She's not a *nothing*."

"Her name is Kristin Faraday." Mrs. Norton's voice was cool but firm. "Martin knows her. He'll tell me more about her history tomorrow."

"What do we do if she returns?"

"We invite her in. We offer her a nice carbonated beverage and tell her about the café's daily special."

Worry remained on Alice Poe's face.

"She's a child," Mrs. Norton said. "Her presence is unexpected, certainly, but not a major concern. If something changes, I'll deal with her."

Chapter Thirteen

The adding machine's motor whirred and an inch of paper spit from its mouth. Lowering her reading glasses, Becky gave the numbers a glance. Resting the glasses atop her head, she rubbed at her tired eyes.

"How 'bout this one?" Sitting beside her, Kristin rubbed a yellow marker over the newspaper on the table.

"Tell me."

She squinted at the tiny print. "'X-sharp 4-door with m-g-t-f, all p-w-r, 158K, $850 o-b-o.'"

"It has 158,000 miles on it?"

"But it's extra sharp. If it's in good condition, those could be very gentle miles."

"I don't know. That's a large number of very gentle miles."

"Probably a little old lady who only drove it to Sunday school," Kristin said. "Church miles don't count. Hawkins is always talking about the Bible to me. I'm sure that's in there somewhere."

"Because the Honda Civic was the car of choice in Biblical times."

"Exactly what I was thinking. What is 'm-g-t-f', anyway?"

"Much grief to follow? Honey, it doesn't matter. You don't have eight hundred and fifty dollars."

"O-b-o, remember? Five hundred and eighty-nine dollars might well be the best offer. Then I'm the proud owner of a sweet Honda Civic –"

"– driven during the days of David and Goliath, with an odometer to match," Becky interrupted.

"I'd have my own wheels, that's the thing."

"That's another issue. At that price, the car will almost certainly need new tires. And then there's maintenance costs, registration fees, insurance...."

"What's your point?"

"It's going to cost more than you expect. You don't think so but it will. Everything in the universe always cost more than you expect and you try, and you try –" Becky thumped her mechanical pencil against the head of the adding machine "– and it's never enough."

"Ohhh-kay."

"Sorry, honey." She let a whistle of air escape from her nose. "Just another one of your mother's monthly meltdowns."

"Try and say that five times fast." Kristin folded the newspaper in half. "Bills, huh?"

"Things have been a little slow at the gallery. Never mind. We'll get by. We always do."

Kristin tucked the paper under one arm. "Mom?"

"Hmmm?" Becky returned the reading glasses to the bridge of her nose. Shaking a bank statement from its envelope, she bent toward the adding machine.

"I saw something today. Something – weird."

"Were you at the mall?"

"What?"

"You said you and Hawkins were going to the mall today."

77

"That's not the point."

"Is a new store opening?"

"No. I mean, what are you trying to say? Not everything in my life revolves around shopping."

Becky tapped a finger over the adding machine's keys. "Shopping or boys, college or a job. And, lately, cars. I've pretty much covered the play list, right?"

"Yes. Yes, I guess you did," Kristin said, sarcasm coloring her words. "That's everything I'm interested in. Shopping, boys, a job. Cars."

"Oh, and there's the cable show you like."

She threw her hands in the air in disbelief. The newspaper fluttered to the ground as she stomped off.

"Honey?" Becky called out. "You forgot to tell me about the new store."

From upstairs, Kristin's bedroom door slammed shut.

* * *

It was dark outside before Becky folded the bank statement inside its envelope. She'd spent the last three hours chasing a twenty-four dollar and fifteen cent discrepancy in her checking account. Finally, she'd tracked it down. Only then had she remembered the jammed cash register at the supermarket and the debit slip she'd never received.

"No big deal," she told the clerk at the time. Little did she know.

It wouldn't have been a big deal, she reflected, clicking off the office lights and closing its door, *if you somehow managed to save a few dollars now and then.*

78

Between the credit card bill and the bounced check fees, insolvency beckons. If you keep this up, you'll lose the house.

What will you do then?

She paused in the hallway. From the floor above her, she heard an unfamiliar voice. It was a male voice, speaking in a low tone. It sounded like the words were coming from her daughter's bedroom.

"Kristin?"

She didn't answer. The voice continued to talk, muffled behind the closed door.

Buried in paperwork, did I somehow miss Hawkins, come to visit?

Not this late. It's probably just a television show.

She listened more closely. There weren't any of the usual television sounds: No gunshots, no squealing tires, no weird sci-fi sound effects. The indistinct voice continued speaking into the emptiness.

It was probably her imagination but the disembodied voice seemed to be speaking more urgently. She gripped the stair's railing.

Has to be the television, she thought. *No reason to even check.*

She started up the stairs.

All parents worry about their children. It doesn't matter how old they get. Kristin is still my child and I will forever worry about her.

But not like before. Not like when Rick died. When Rick died, things had gotten truly strange.

"You want to talk paranoid," she muttered. *Lose your husband, lose your mind.* If she hadn't been clinically paranoid during those first terrible months, she'd been close to it.

In those days, it felt as if only she cared whether Kristin lived or died. Becky's parents were long dead but Rick's widowed mother had refused to even touch the baby. Heartbroken over the loss of her only son, she'd died without ever knowing her grandchild.

Gripped by despair, Becky soon began to imagine everyone else felt the same way about her daughter. Her mind clouded with grief, she thought she was the only person who would ever love Kristin. *Could* ever love Kristin.

In reflection, she supposed she'd had a kind of mental breakdown. Since those early days, Kristin had grown into a lovely young woman. She'd found some good friends; not many, admittedly, but some, and that was enough. She had a social life, dated, had gone steady a time or two. She'd even danced at the Junior Prom, something Becky had never done.

In short, her daughter had lived her life. It was a good life if not an exciting one.

Becky felt she'd had enough excitement for a lifetime. She didn't want any more of it tonight.

She pressed her ear against the bedroom door. From inside, a man spoke, his words maddeningly unintelligible. If her daughter was in the room with him, she was silent.

Forgive me, kiddo. I try to give you your space, I do. I almost never go into your bedroom.

This doesn't count as snooping. This is legitimate parental concern.

Squeezing the handle, she pushed the door open.

Hallway light spilled into the dark bedroom. Dressed in her jeans and t-shirt, Kristin lay asleep on her bed. One of her sandals dangled perilously from her left foot. The other shoe had fallen to the floor.

From inside the darkness, a man said, "Tell me there are no werewolves, I'll agree with you. If you don't believe in the Loch Ness Monster, if you question the existence of Bigfoot, you'll get no argument from me. But tell me there's no such thing as ghosts and I'll call you a fool."

Entering the room, Becky touched the space bar on the computer's keyboard. Its monitor brightened and a dark-haired man glared out at her from the screen. Below the man's image, subtitles on the screen read: *Dr. Marc Ericks, Liefeld College.*

Ericks said, "These aren't kindly ghosts, concerned with your well-being. Your beloved Uncle Burt isn't standing beside you, guiding your step. Your sweet Aunt Claudette isn't floating below your ceiling, watching over you."

An overhead light shone down on the professor, accenting the wrinkles under his eyes. From the camera's view, he came across as tired and alone, sitting by himself in an empty room.

Probably had to set up his own camera and lighting, too, Becky thought. *The obsessed can rarely afford to fund a production crew.*

There were print-outs in the computer's paper tray. Picking them up, Becky leafed through them. "Wraiths? The invisible man?"

"Nor are these specters simply misguided souls, trying to find their way to heaven," Ericks continued,

81

tugging at a patch of gray in his beard. "These are creatures without a heart, without a soul. They're evil incarnate. They hunger –"

"Oh, please." Taking the computer's mouse, she turned the machine off. The deluded professor disappeared in mid-sentence.

A fluttering of curtains told her the bedroom window was open. Moving Kristin's plastic Tinkerbelle figurine from the bottom sill, Becky grasped the window's wooden upper rail. She glanced down at the street.

Slight of build and dressed in a woman's full-length tan coat, a figure waited on the sidewalk. The jacket's hood obscured its owner's face. Under Becky's gaze, the stranger walked away, quickly moving out of the circle of light provided by the boulevard's solitary street lamp.

Who was that?

Listening closely, she couldn't hear the stranger's footsteps as she left.

"Great," she told the computer. "Now you've got me seeing ghosts."

Shutting the window firmly, she slid its sash lock closed.

Chapter Fourteen

From Kristin's Diary

What if life is like the old movie, The Matrix?

You take the right pill, you get to believe whatever you want to believe. The same thing everyone else believes. You take the wrong pill and you're lost in Wonderland forever.

One pill makes you larger. One pill makes you small.

This morning, I didn't flush Dr. Ron's pink pill down the toilet. I still have it, safely nestled in the bottom of my jewelry box. My old Disney Mad Hatter pin is lying on top of it, in case Mom decides to take a quick peek through my earrings and necklaces.

Which has never happened, not once in my entire life.

But just because something *hasn't* happened doesn't mean it *can't* happen. Like when I saw the ghost people. Seeing ghost people was definitely a new experience.

Hawk was there, too, and he got angry, mad at the glass asshole, but he didn't see anything unusual about the guy. But the ghost man realized I could tell something was wrong with him. As if he was aware he was a see-through monstrosity and he knew *I* knew but he also knew I wouldn't tell anyone. Like, somehow, he'd come across people like me before.

If I'm reading him correctly, then maybe I don't need to book an immediate return trip to the pastoral grounds of Kendall Sanitarium. Maybe. Because, just when I thought I'd finally figured out all the things that were weird about me, along comes Mr. Glass – sorry, Mr. Locke – to prove me wrong.

Which makes me wonder if I'm wrong about some other things, too. Like taking the pills Dr. Ron ordered.

If I'd been using my medication all along, as my psychiatrist insisted, maybe I'd be normal by now. Because what if there's a process involved? At first, the medication leaves you feeling all fuzzy and wool-headed but, later, you're turned into a good, upstanding citizen, a little dull of thought and slow to respond but no longer seeing crazy-ass crap that can't/shouldn't/doesn't exist?

That's not exactly the life I crave but there are days when I'd settle for it.

Somewhere along the line, I must have taken the wrong pill. But is the pink pill the one I really need?

How do I escape Wonderland?

*

About my Mad Hatter pin: I bought it about three years ago, when the Debate Team traveled to Southern California for the Nationals and everyone went to Disneyland. We all acted like we were too cool for some overcrowded theme park, and we were, truly, but everybody showed up at the front gates, anyway. The Nationals were a total bust, only Cleve Kisner won anything, but it was fun, anyway.

At the gift shop, paying three times what a chain store would charge, I bought the Mad Hatter pin. I stuck it on my t-shirt on my way home and Mom spotted it the instant I stepped off the bus. She had a total meltdown. She acted like I was advertising my past, rather than properly hiding it from the world.

As if everybody in Winterhaven didn't already know about me.

"The gift shop had to have other pins," Mom said. "Why didn't you get Alice? Or the Cheshire Cat?"

Her exact words.

I know this because I wrote everything down the night I came home. It's maybe the best thing about keeping a diary. If you put in an entry every three or four days, like I do, you can go back and see the things that happened to you. Your memories are right there.

I flip through the pages and I see all of the stuff I wrote about Dr. Ron. The other stuff, too. The paragraphs about melting faces. The dreams I've experienced. All of the pills I've flushed.

In other words, the complete and total chronicle of my unbalanced life.

This comes to mind because, sitting at my desk, staring out of my bedroom window, I notice Tinkerbelle has somehow moved off of my window sill. Miss Belle, with your wings so pretty, did you somehow fly down to my end table last night?

Or did someone put you on the counter and forget? Was someone in my room?

I don't remember turning my computer off, either. I'm sure I left the window open. Pretty sure, anyway.

85

This is supposed to be my personal space. Years ago, Mom promised she wouldn't enter this room without my permission. Years ago, I believed her.

Fuck.

What use is a journal if you think someone else is going to read what you've written? You can't be totally honest if you suspect someone is spying on you.

I love having a place to share my thoughts, my best and worst, most wonderful and awful memories, because I can't share them anywhere else. Now I wonder if I dare write another line, another sentence.

There are hundreds of pages here, hundreds of entries, but, if somebody finds my words, none of it will remain secret. The cops will be called, just like at school, and I'll be back in the embrace of Dr. Ron before I get a chance to have a real life.

I wrote about everything here. My first kiss. My first date, my first boyfriend, my first...

Everything.

Fuck, fuck, *fuck*.

*

So, what do I do now? Do I hide my diary and hope no one finds it? Do I find a box and lock it up? Or do I destroy it, feeding my memories into the shredder, sheet by sheet?

I'd like another option, please. One that acknowledges my right to a little privacy. But that's never going to happen, not unless I get my own place.

I can't wait to leave here. Can't wait to leave Winterhaven. So that's what I'm going to do.

But, first, I need to find out who the glass people are. Find out why they're here. What they're doing. Because they scare me, more than a little, and I'm the only one who can tell what they are.

Whatever that is.

Unless, of course, none of what I see is real and I'm completely, totally batshit.

I guess that might be good to know, too....

Chapter Fifteen

At daybreak, Kristin walked to the café. The front of the building was closed and its upper windows were dark.

She abandoned the sidewalk for the dirt lane that served as the café's back alley. A new fence blocked the back of the structure, its wooden slats spaced in six-foot sections with a heavy metal post supporting each of the divisions.

This is new, she realized. *Since when did Piotrowski's get a fence?*

The structure was built from Douglas fir, the same inexpensive wood her mother had once used to build a rabbit hut. Untreated, the rabbit hut had rotted after two hard winters.

This crappy stain job won't protect the wood for long. Maybe the ghost people don't care.

Exactly how long do they intend to stay in Winterhaven, anyway?

The double-gate to the fence was open. A truck was parked inside the yard, its sides emblazoned with stylized images of apples and carrots. The truck's driver wheeled a loaded dolly down a metal ramp. Walking beside him was another one of the crystalline men.

Stepping closer to the fence, Kristin peered between two of the slats. This glass man was bigger than the other ghost people she'd seen. His powerful arms swung easily

88

from a thick barrel chest. His head was square-shaped, with thick lips and a heavy nose. The driver spoke in a low voice to him.

The big man barked a short, loud laugh. "Just like a woman, right?" his voice boomed out.

The receiving door opened. Martin Piotrowski gestured at the driver as the glass man plodded forward, pretending not to see the older man. Drawing closer, he threw his wide left shoulder into Martin. The blow knocked him backwards, causing him to hit the door frame and slide to the ground.

"Careful, old-timer," the glass man said as the driver pushed his cargo inside.

Martin spoke softly, the bigger man looming over him. Finally, the man extended an arm to help him to his feet. When he stood, the glass man clapped him on his back, a little too roughly.

"My first name?" the glass man said. "It's Martin. Same as you, eh?"

Schhhct! Finishing his lie, a clear layer fell over the big man's mouth. A second layer dropped over it and then a third, falling atop one another like so many glass dominoes.

"I don't like to use the name much." The words reverberated strangely, as if the big man was speaking from inside a box. "You hear 'Martin', it makes you think of somebody weak and useless. Somebody soft. Every time I say the name, I want to puke in disgust."

Schhhct! His mouth reappeared.

"Here's what I think," he continued, "my own personal theory if you will."

He moved closer to Martin, pressing his chest forward until it crowded the smaller man. "Anybody uses your first name, they don't respect you. When you're in charge, when you're feared, people use your last name. They know to call you 'mister'." He brought his face down until he was nose-to-nose with the café's former owner. "You want to keep me happy, call me Mr. Brass."

Martin blinked at him, speechless.

"Let's get going, Marty," Mr. Brass said in his deep voice. "Those cartons of lettuce aren't going to put themselves into storage."

* * *

Sitting on the curb opposite the café, Kristin sipped at a diet cola.

Something's the matter with you, girl. You've spent your entire morning within viewing distance of what used to be the best restaurant in Winterhaven – and, when lunch time comes, you walk a mile-and-a-half to Bill's Burgers to get a burger and fries. You don't even like the food at Bill's Burgers.

Her mind teased, *Like it better than the new management at Piotrowski's Café, though, don't you?*

She opened her cell phone. Almost instantly, the *No Network* message appeared on screen. Strange. Back when she worked at the café, she'd always been able to get cell reception.

"Exactly why aren't you working?" she asked the cell phone. "Is there something wrong with your satellite – or something wrong with *here*?"

90

From behind her, a voice said, "Did you eat lead chips as a child?"

Startled, Kristin closed her phone. Putting one well-manicured hand on the concrete curb, Liz Wheeler sat beside her. "Phone call from Mister Imaginary Friend?"

"I – I...."

"Piotrowski's isn't hiring. I've checked."

"That's – no. That's not... it's not why I'm here."

"It totally is," Liz said. "You're scoping them out. It's obvious."

"Did you really ask for a job application?"

"I didn't make a special trip here just to get an app, if that's what you're wondering. I happened to be here so I asked."

"Last year, you told me you'd never be a waitress," Kristin said. "All the grease was bad for your perfect complexion. It would take the curl out of your gorgeous red hair."

"I said I had a perfect complexion?"

"Inferred."

"Regrets." Liz sighed. "Last year, I had an allowance. That's gone until I somehow get into college." She waved a hand over her clothing. "Last season's designer jeans. The cute emerald sandals, so I don't tower over every guy I meet? Asian knock-offs. This to-die-for Brazilian blouse? It's a ramie blend and it wrinkles every time I bend."

"You must not bend very much, then."

"Bonus points: It was hand sewn by a spoiled redhead with a perfect complexion."

"I never said you were spoiled."

"I am, though. Was."

91

Kristin said, "If you aren't job-hunting, why are you here?"

"Can't I just be curb-hopping with my best girl buddy?"

"No." When Liz looked hurt, she said, "You're not a curb kind of girl. You're more of a muscle car kind of girl."

"Not when Nana Beggio takes my keys."

"Bad Nana Beggio."

"If you had a car, you could drive me around."

"Yeah, right."

"No closer than before?"

"Farther, if anything. Yesterday, I went on a spending spree and bought myself some chapstick."

"Spendthrift," Liz said. "If you must know, I'm hunting for Mouser."

"Your grandmother's cat?"

"Disappeared again. Gone for two days and Nana is going nuts. It's only a cat, right? A mean cat."

"You like Mouser."

"Not –" Liz's mouth blurred as a vague cloud of softly freckled skin covered it "– so much." At the end of the sentence, her lips snapped back in focus.

"Liar."

"Didn't lie. Considered lying. *Almost* lied. Can't find the damned cat, though. In this part of the city, there's almost always a few strays wandering around." She viewed the area around them. "Funny. Not a single wee beastie to be seen."

Kristin sniffed the air. "I blame your perfume."

"You know," Liz said, bringing her wrist to her nose, "so do I."

92

Chapter Sixteen

Alice Poe stood behind the front blinds, her fingers forcing a gap between the plastic sleeves. Miss Sweet's cane tapped over the tiled flooring as she approached.

"I hate this stick," Miss Sweet said. To emphasize her point, she thumped the red-brown pole's rubber base against the floor.

Alice Poe remained at the window.

"The Bubinga wood is too heavy for comfort," Miss Sweet continued. "The carved head fits poorly underneath my hand." She rolled her twisted fingers over the jackal's skull.

"You'll be rid of it soon enough," Alice Poe said in a distracted tone.

Miss Sweet pushed beside her to follow her gaze. "It's her."

"I know."

"Nasty thing." She scraped the long nail of her index finger over a vein in the wooden head of the cane.

"She's just sitting there. Staring at us."

"Do you think she knows?"

"Mr. Locke says she doesn't." Anxiety touched her words. "Mr. Brass isn't concerned but he's the hungriest of us. When you're hungry, you make mistakes."

"What does Mrs. Norton say?"

"Mrs. Norton isn't afraid of anything."

"You haven't shared as much time with her as I have," Miss Sweet said. "In the beginning, the early days, she had her fears. One such as this might have frightened her."

"Now?"

"If she has her fears, she doesn't share them."

With her free hand, Alice Poe touched the chain around her neck. Her fingers found its ankh pendant and she played with it nervously. "Is it true that only the pure can be tasted?"

"Their kind has purity at birth. Not for long after."

Alice Poe pushed a hungry tongue between her colorless lips. Miss Sweet's eyes narrowed. "The pure are not for the likes of you."

"Nor you," Alice Poe responded, spitting her words.

Miss Sweet ignored the sting in her words. She smiled at a distant memory, sending a cascade of wrinkles rising up her empty face. "The ones who get tasted – the little ones – they rarely live, you know. They're abandoned, neglected... lost."

Alice Poe brightened at this thought.

"A fall from a crib, forgotten in a tub, left in a too hot car," Miss Sweet continued. "The parents reassure themselves that they tried. People can only do so much. They're not to blame."

"Accidents happen."

"Yes. Yes, they do."

"What of this one?" Alice Poe gestured toward the street outside. "Why is she still here?"

"Yes. Well." The pleasure leaked from Miss Sweet's voice. "Even in our world, mysteries abound."

At the sound of footsteps, they stopped talking. Mrs. Norton entered, stopping in front of Alice Poe. "I haven't been able to find your Mr. Locke."

Alice Poe rubbed her thumb furiously over the face of the silver ankh.

"He wanders," Mrs. Norton said. "He wins no favor when he shirks his duties. Mr. Brass is furious."

"I'll find him."

"It would be best if you did so quickly." To Miss Sweet, she asked, "Is your room ready for customers?"

"I have the crystals and new candles."

"It's not enough. In a place like this, a small town, they want incense and astrological signs. The Chinese calendar. Gypsy clothing. When our customers come upstairs to see a fortune teller, they expect to find something they might have seen in the movies."

"Fools."

"You've wasted enough time for today." Mrs. Norton clapped her hands together sharply. "Both of you, finish your chores. We have our grand opening tomorrow."

Chapter Seventeen

His dead wife said, "I don't know, Howard. I'm not sure I like this new woman."

"She's a good person," the Reverend Hawkins told her. "She comes to Bible Study every week. She's at both of the Sunday services."

"Then why doesn't she take you as you are? Why do you have to change yourself?"

"A small change. A cosmetic change. I did it to please myself."

"Always pleasing yourself," Eustacia said. She frowned and her shattered cheek sunk in on itself. "She's been divorced. You know what I think about divorce."

"We've had this discussion."

Eustacia held her frown. She fixed her remaining green eye on her husband.

"I like Ms. Parkes. I hope to see more of her."

"I don't know why I bother," she said in her snippiest voice. "You always do what you want, anyway."

In death, as in life, she was so easily offended. Sometimes he didn't know what to say.

"It's Gideon I worry about," she continued. "Who knows if she'll be good for him?"

He took a deep breath. "Gideon's a man now, Eustacia. He's not a child, anymore."

"Don't be silly."

"It's true. Remember the last time we talked. Try to remember, darling."

He could almost see her thought process as she tried to knit her memories together. Even if she remembered, it wouldn't last. He reminded her of Gideon's age with almost every nocturnal visit. For her, time remained frozen at the moment of the accident.

Her ruined face studied him. "Is she prettier than me?"

Poor Eustacia. "No one is prettier than you."

His response pleased her. "What's the woman's first name again?"

"Brenda."

"Brenda," she said, as if she'd bitten into something distasteful. "What are your plans for this – Brenda?"

"I don't have any plans. Not now, not yet. Eventually, I may ask her out on a date."

"Take her on a picnic."

His heart sank.

"Maybe on a Friday. The parishioners don't bother you on Fridays." Her shredded face regarded him. "You might pack a lunch, carry it in our wicker basket. A little cheese, a loaf of bread."

"Stop it, Eustacia."

"A bottle of wine, too. What harm could it do?"

From somewhere in the clouds behind her, a telephone rang.

"You still drink wine, don't you, Howard?"

"You know I don't. You know I've stopped."

The telephone rang.

"A little too late, wouldn't you say?"

97

"I'm so sorry." He was, too. He would forever be sorry for what he'd done.

"There's something else we need to talk about."

The telephone rang.

"There's evil in Winterhaven," she said, "It's a preacher's job to watch for the sinful. How could you have been so careless?"

The telephone!

His eyes came open. Reaching out in the darkness, his hand found the phone's receiver. "Hello?"

"Reverend?" It was the sad, almost mournful, voice of Ed Whitlock. "Sorry to call so early."

The Reverend felt for the alarm clock. He moved its glowing digital face so he could see it more clearly.

It was nearly five in the morning. Early enough to start the day.

What a blessing.

"It's my mother," Ed said. "She fell at the nursing home last night. The doctor's ordered x-rays, he thinks she's broken a hip."

"Go."

"There's nobody to cover me."

"Don't let it bother you," he said into the receiver. "Family comes first. Galilee Church will still be standing when you get back."

He hung up the phone. His heart was starting to slow. His pajamas felt wet and sticky.

"Sinner," he told himself. "Sinner."

He hated these nightmares, but he'd earned them. If he never slept well again, he couldn't complain.

It was nothing less than he deserved.

98

* * *

His father with the too-brown hair stood at the lectern. He adjusted his reading glasses before examining the index cards on the face of the podium. "After the morning prayer, everyone takes their seat, the choir goes into 'All Glory to the Father' –"

"All glo-ry to the Father be!" Hawkins shouted. He squeezed the rag in his hand. Soapy water dripped into the bucket at his feet.

A flicker of irritation passed over Reverend Hawkins' face. "Tina Flores will announce the results of the bake sale –" He scanned the index card in his hand. "Two hundred and forty dollars. Not bad."

"*Hal*-lelujah!" Hawkins cried. Putting the damp rag against the glossy finish of the red oak pew, he wiped it along the back of the long bench.

His father removed his reading glasses. "Having fun, Gideon?"

"Yes, sir. I mean... no, sir."

"I know you'd planned to see Kristin today," the Reverend said. "I'm aware your time together is limited. To my mind, this is not necessarily a bad thing."

Rather than respond, Hawkins dropped his rag into the bucket of soapy water.

"If you're going to be a preacher, a man of God, you need to learn prioritization. Your wishes are frequently served last."

"I think I understand that."

"So, when the maintenance man calls to say he'll be out of town for the rest of the week, someone has to sweep

99

the floors. Someone has to clean the pews. All too often, this 'someone' ends up being the congregation's leader."

Or his son, Hawkins thought.

"We're clear on this? If I decide to practice my sermon, I'm not going to have to listen to a laugh track?"

"Not with one of your sermons," Hawkins muttered. Scooping the rag from the gray bucket of water, he twisted it forcefully. He rubbed its face along the curved edge of the pew's side support.

His father bent his head down, scrutinizing his notes. The light mounted over the lectern reflected off of the brown mulch that was serving as his hair.

Hawkins didn't know why the color change bothered him so much. It was only hair, no matter what his father did to it. Keratinized protein filament, if Greg Cohen, his old chemistry teacher, was to be believed.

Howard Hawkins own protein used to be silver-white, a good color for a preacher. Now it was some kind of burnt umber.

A good color for a used car salesman.

He'd obviously done the dye job himself. It was just as obvious that he'd made the change because of the church's newest parishioner. Brenda Parkes was new to the congregation and to Winterhaven. She was a middle-aged divorcee, all soft curves and bright smiles. Her hair was brown and, because of her age, it was probably dyed, too. On her, the color seemed right.

Hawkins kind of liked her. Still, it bugged him to see his father suddenly buying new clothes, changing his hair, and pretending as if everything was normal.

100

Maybe if he mentioned her, just once, in all of our hours together. Would it kill him to share his feelings with me?

Speak to me, he thought. *Don't lecture me. Don't preach. Talk man-to-man, father-to-son.*

Fat chance.

"Almost done?" his father asked from the podium. Straightening the index cards, he pulled a rubber band around them.

"Getting there," Hawkins said. "See you at home."

"I'll be late." Opening his briefcase, his father slid his practice materials into an inner sleeve. "I think I'll get a few reps in."

"You're going to the gym?"

"'Exercise thyself into godliness'."

"Oh, yeah. I remember seeing the slogan over at 24 Hour Fitness."

Swinging the briefcase, his father left the podium. Humming lightly, he went past his son and through the large Gothic front door. Hawkins saw him pass a pedestrian and climb into his car just before the door *snicked* shut.

Hawkins remained inside the doorway. The pedestrian on the walkway was familiar to him. He'd seen him before.

It was the guy at Piotrowski's, the one who'd bullied Kristin. The one who called her 'meat'.

What's his name again?

"Mr. Locke." Saying the man's name, a bizarre feeling washed over him. He felt a sudden need to hide. He wanted to crawl under one of the pews and curl

101

himself into a ball. That way, when Mr. Locke entered the church, he couldn't find him.

Grow a pair, he told himself.

Remember Hunter Davis, senior year? He was a lot like this guy. Just as aggressive but bigger. Chunked-up biceps, same kind of strut when he walked. What did you do when he got in your face?

You didn't back down. You stood up to him. Kicked his butt, that's what you did.

Hawkins shoved at the heavy front door, stepping onto the front landing. "What do you want?"

Out on the walkway, two fingers of each hand tucked into the top of his pants pockets, Mr. Locke grinned. "Are you talking to me?"

"You know who I'm talking to."

"No," he said. "No, I don't. I was on a walk, strolling past this lovely church, when the door suddenly flew open and you came out, shouting. Have we met?"

The anger drained from Hawkins' face, quickly replaced by embarrassment.

I'm such a jackass. He doesn't even remember me.

Taking his left hand from his pocket, the other man rubbed at his face as if something was bothering him. His fingers played over his mouth.

He let his hand drop. "Wait, I think I'm wrong. Maybe I *do* know you. You're the kid who was at my restaurant."

"Sorry. Just – sorry."

"You were staring at me."

"That's not...." He couldn't finish the sentence. In its own way, it was true enough.

"You told me to screw myself."

102

"I never said that."

"That's okay. It didn't make me mad." His hips pistoned awkwardly as Locke came up the concrete path. "You can stare at me if you want."

Hawkins retreated. "That is *not* what I want."

Mr. Locke said, "You're not very friendly. I thought the God-fearing were supposed to be friendly."

"I apologize, all right? For coming out here. For shouting. For... for staring, if that's what you think happened." He reached for the large cast iron door handle behind him. "I've got to get back to work."

"Do you want to know a secret?"

Hawkins clutched at the handle more tightly. "No."

"I can whisper it in your ear if you'd like."

"Mr. Locke!" a female voice cried out. A woman ran toward them, her cotton dress too large for her frame. Her golden bracelet bounced along her thin wrist as she raced along the sidewalk.

With regret in his voice, Mr. Locke said, "Alice Poe."

"Where have you been?" The woman's watery blue eyes went past him to Hawkins. Unhappiness pinched her tight face.

"I was on a walk."

"Mrs. Norton wants you to return. Now."

"Mrs. Norton, Mrs. Norton. I'm tired of hearing about the wants and demands of our Mrs. Norton."

"You dare not say that."

"Not to Mrs. Norton," he told her lightly. Allowing himself to be tugged away, he looked over his shoulder as he left. "Young Master Hawkins?"

"What?"

"We'll share our secrets later. In private, just you and me. Okay?"

Hawkins watched the pair go from sidewalk to asphalt and then around the corner. Headed, he supposed, back to Piotrowski's Café.

Back to Mrs. Norton.

Entering the church, he closed the door. *That was definitely kinda creepy.*

Later, he wondered: *How did Mr. Locke know my name?*

Chapter Eighteen

An hour after the café opened, she saw him still there, sitting at a corner table. Small, alone and largely forgotten, Martin Piotrowski desperately wanted to be of some use to someone, somewhere.

It's a pity I can't give him the opportunity, Mrs. Norton thought.

Alice Poe stopped at his table to fill his water glass. Knowing Mrs. Norton was watching, she tipped her head in the direction of another solitary customer. Sitting at Table Seven, this one slurped pasta into his mouth, letting it slide over his chin before it disappeared.

This particular customer didn't seem like the kind to welcome company before his plate was empty. Mrs. Norton decided she'd deal with him soon enough. First, she needed to send Martin on his way.

Glass in hand, he waved in her direction. When he did, Alice Poe left him for the next table. Mr. Locke stalked sullenly behind her, a busboy's blue apron tied around his waist.

"Something else to eat, Martin?" Mrs. Norton asked. "A slice of pie, perhaps?"

He patted at his stomach. "The linguisa was more than enough."

"Do I get your review?"

"Good, the meal was good," he said. "Add a little chopped marjoram with the peppers and onion, it would be even better. It's a subtle touch but the customers love it. I can show Mr. Brass how it's done, if you'd like."

"You know what they say about too many cooks, my dear."

"I'll bring the recipe tomorrow. Just in case." Pulling out his wallet, he dropped a bill on the table. When Mrs. Norton protested, he raised his hand. "You can't afford to give away food. Not when you're starting out."

"Money isn't everything."

"It is in the restaurant business." He stood up from his chair. "I know a few things about running a restaurant. You agree?"

"Martin...."

He lowered his voice. "Piotrowski's Café failed once. I don't want you to know such heartbreak."

"I won't," Mrs. Norton said.

"You can't be sure. After all, this is your grand opening, Constance. The grand opening and there are empty tables around me."

"Two empty tables, Martin. Three, once you leave. It's hardly time to file bankruptcy papers."

"The café has to generate more income to survive," he said. "You've got to serve something besides lunch. If you add breakfast to your menu –"

"No."

"Two eggs, two pieces of toast, a slice of bacon. It costs pennies, it brings in dollars. If I'd served breakfast, I'd still be in business."

Mr. Locke circled around them. Removing the table's dirty dishes, he slid them into a black plastic tub.

"We can talk about this later. For now, go home. Rest."

"You'll do what's best." Martin's tone implied only he truly knew what was best.

"With your help, I'm certain we'll muddle through." Placing a hand on his shoulder, she pressed gently to encourage him to move toward the exit.

Slowly, reluctantly, he left.

Mr. Locke stayed at the small, circular table. "Why does he call you 'Constance'?"

"The invoices we receive are made out to Constance Norton. Martin made an assumption."

"It's not your name."

"He thinks it is."

"Constance Norton." The thought amused him. When he smiled, his cheekbones became more pronounced.

He really is beautiful, Mrs. Norton thought. *Such a shame.*

Beauty was so rare it attracted interest. The interest of others was, now and forever, unwanted. She'd do nothing about it yet. In a few months, if Mr. Locke hadn't learned to disguise his looks, she'd take action.

It would be rash to act too soon. Better to wait until the others realized his appearance was a detriment to their future, to the opportunities awaiting them. Mrs. Norton had survived this long because she knew when to let others think her ideas were their own.

If and when the time came to address the issue in a physical manner, she'd let Mr. Brass assist her. He enjoyed those kinds of things.

Pulling a cloth from his waistband, Mr. Locke swiped at the splattering of sauce on the table. "The old meat is right. The café isn't busy enough."

"It's our first day."

"If every table was full, we'd have more to choose from. As it is, hardly anyone has gone upstairs."

"It's only our first day."

She knew he wanted to offer another protest. His courage faltered and he pretended to be distracted by the cloth in his hand. "We could serve breakfast, though. It would be easy."

"Do you know who comes to breakfast?"

"Customers."

"Busy people," she said. "People in a hurry, grabbing a bite before they go to work. We don't want that kind of clientele."

He was still lost, she could tell. He thought he knew so much. It chafed him to discover there were more things left to learn.

Pretty or not, he was becoming tiresome. It would be a pleasure to scar his lovely face.

"Busy people are people with responsibilities," she said. "People who will be missed. They have families in need of their paycheck, co-workers who count on their presence. When something happens to someone who is needed, alarms are sounded." She tipped her head toward Table Seven. "We want the lonely. We want the dispossessed. We want customers who have nothing better to do in the middle of their day than to go to an adequate restaurant in a strangled little town."

"Because they mean nothing to anybody. Less than nothing."

"Because no one cares about them," she corrected him. "No one except for us."

Mr. Locke tossed his cloth into the tub of dirty dishes.

"In the last few years, with information ever more available, I've had to learn to be patient," Mrs. Norton said. "In time, you'll learn to be patient, too."

Mr. Locke appeared doubtful.

"Finish your duties. I need to see a customer."

* * *

He said his name was Kevin Zhou. In his professional life, he'd made his living in one of the oldest of the professions.

He was a traveling salesman.

"For years, I traveled coast-to-coast. Medical supplies. Colonoscopes, mostly," he said, as if a discussion of colonoscopes was appropriate for casual conversation with a stranger. "There's some serious money to be made in the medical field, I'll tell you."

If he'd kept any of his money, it wasn't apparent on first inspection. His worn camel hair sport coat was folded sloppily over the top of the empty chair at his table. He wore a nondescript cream-colored shirt with plastic buttons; the shirt's tail was tucked into a pair of unfashionable brown slacks. If she was a betting woman – and she, most definitely, was not – Mrs. Norton would have wagered on Zhou's choice of footwear. Beneath the table's white cloth, she was certain she'd find him wearing a pair of cotton-nylon socks tucked into scuffed department store shoes.

Still and all. He was retired but not enfeebled. He lacked a dining companion and didn't wear a wedding ring. He had possibilities.

Dabbing at his mouth with a napkin, Zhou asked, "Are you the diner's owner?"

"My family and I."

"You work as a waitress, then?"

"I'm the manager."

"Yet you wait tables."

"Alice Poe is our waitress," she said. "When business demands, we all step in to help."

"Wise, very wise," Zhou responded. "Piotrowski killed his business, you know, paying for staff. Two waitresses, a cook's assistant, and God knows who else. Anyone who asked for an application, he gave them a job. And to what end? Out of business in less than three years' time."

"At least his name lives on."

"He made good food, I'll give him that much." Zhou dropped his napkin to the table. "Your chef isn't as talented. The pasta was overcooked, the sauce tasted bland. I'm surprised I was able to finish my lunch." He picked up his bill and toyed with it.

She'd seen Zhou's kind before. They'd finish their meal, leave not a crumb uneaten, and then utter some vague complaint in the hope their bill would be discounted. Thinking they were clever when all they really were was annoying.

"Perhaps I can offer a dessert in way of apology," she told the round-bellied man.

110

Retreating through the rear door, she went into the kitchen. Opening the large commercial refrigerator at the back of the building, she stepped inside.

The remains of the afternoon's two-crust apple pie waited for her. Miss Sweet believed her particular combination of fresh sliced apples, ground cinnamon, and white sugar was a panacea for every mortal complaint. It was almost too good. If demand grew for the treat, it would be removed from the menu.

For now, the colonoscope salesman could enjoy its pleasures. Transferring a thick wedge of the pie onto a dessert plate, she closed the door behind her.

Without saying a word, Zhou pushed his fork through the pie's flaky crust. His expression changed as his mouth closed over the treat. "This is fresh. Not commercial."

"Naturally."

He offered no further conversation, his fork clicking against the plate as it swept away the rest of the pie.

Mrs. Norton pulled the empty chair back from the table. Avoiding her customer's sport coat, she sat on edge of the seat. "Zhou is a Chinese name, isn't it?"

He nodded, removing the fork from his mouth. A flake of golden crust dangled from his lower lip.

"I knew a Zhou family once. Pig farmers, from the Sichuan Province."

"You've been to China?"

"Hundreds of years ago. Or so it feels at times." She rested her hand upon his forearm. "I hope you don't have to run off."

The fork in Zhou's hand wobbled. Incredibly, he blushed.

111

She said, "All those years ago, back when China and I were both so much younger, I found a most interesting curio in the Hualong Valley. Do you know of the area?"

"It's in the Songpan mountains."

"Exactly," Mrs. Norton said. "You really should see what I found. It's interesting, so very special. I think you'll be amazed."

"Amazed?" The thought pleased him. "For something amazing, I might spare a moment."

"Wonderful." She rose from the chair. "It's upstairs."

Belatedly, Zhou climbed to his feet. Mrs. Norton went ahead of him, confident he'd follow after her.

By the time he reached the stairway, she was already on the second floor's upper landing. His gaze traveled up the stairway to find her.

"Join me, Mr. Zhou," she said. "Come and see our little piece of magic."

Chapter Nineteen

Propped up by an oversized pillow and loosely covered by a lavender sheet, Susannah Guitierrez rested on the living room sofa. Her warm brown eyes were slightly unfocused as a pleasantly empty expression played about her features.

What a waste of time, Becky thought, the bristles of her paint brush skating over the rectangle of hardwood. *This painting will never, ever sell.*

I'm not just wasting my time, I'm wasting Susannah's time. I'm wasting my supplies.

Once she finished the piece, she'd be lucky to give it away. Susannah wouldn't want it. Her townhouse walls were crowded with photographs. Should she decide, one fine day, to hang a painting in her home, it wouldn't be *this* painting. This painting wouldn't appeal to her at all.

Will it appeal to anyone? Lowering her paintbrush, Becky rested its handle against her hip.

Trying to consider the painting objectively, she admitted it wasn't remotely realistic. With so many bursts of different colors on the board, an outside observer might question if her subject was even human. Instead of calling it, "Portrait of S. Guitierrez", she should have named it, "Explosion at the Paint Factory".

She pressed her brush to her pallet into a circle of Cremnitz white. *So why do I feel so happy?*

Because... well, because.

No, "because" isn't an answer. Try a little harder.

Because I'm not doing this for the money, she decided. *No one commissioned it. I'm not expecting anyone to buy it. It's not important if anyone else likes it.*

This one is for me. No reason to even send it to the gallery.

A mental stab struck at her with the last thought. If Larry at the Centerville Gallery saw the painting, he'd have a heart attack. In Lincoln City's Centerville Square, abstract art didn't sell.

"Abstract art is worthless," Larry declared, not five months ago. "Who wants it? It doesn't mean anything."

We'll have to agree to disagree, Larry.

These monstrous splashes of color symbolized more than a portrait of her friend. The slashes of her brush were an emotional response to Becky's own feelings about age and loss. Susannah was far removed from the young woman she'd first met all those years ago and Becky herself hated to discover new wrinkles reflected in her mirror. Someone, somewhere, needed to shout out against the injustice of life's losses. To cry out at the lurking presence of death.

Do not go gentle into that good night. Not if I have any choice, anyway.

She peeked over the top of her painting. "Getting tired?"

"Tired of what? Lying here?"

Gathering the sheet around her breasts, Susannah leaned forward. "Have you been to the new café?"

"It's not so new from what I've heard."

"You've heard right," Susannah said. "Step inside and you'd swear Martin was still running the place. Same

114

tables, same decorations. You'd think someone would have had the good taste to replace that God-awful flocked wallpaper. I almost expected to see Chandra Piotrowski at the cash register."

"Poor Chandra."

"Poor Chandra, my ass," Susannah said. "She probably ran off with the lifeguard from the Y."

"Chandra, hooking up with twenty-three-year-old Mike 'Muscles' Morley? You can't be serious."

"If only it were true. There might be hope for the rest of us." Pointing her painted toenails, she pushed her feet into the bejeweled sandals sitting at the base of the sofa. Having posed for almost ninety minutes, this was her gentle reminder that she'd grown bored with it.

Becky knew better than to ask for more time. Once she made up her mind, Susannah grew restless. A fidgety model was of no use at all. "You were talking about the restaurant."

"There's a man in the kitchen, you can tell. The meat in my casserole had been chopped to death. Pieces so small, it could have been anything."

"Cow, horse, llama...." Becky wiped at the brush, cleaning the paint from it.

The sheet wrapped around her, Susannah hobbled over to the side chair where she'd dropped her clothing. "Martin was there. He told me a little secret."

"About Chandra?"

She waved her hand dismissively. "About the family that leased the café." Dropping the sheet, she wiggled into a pair of capris. "They live upstairs of the dining area, you know. All five of them." She pulled a knitted sweater over

115

her head. "In the smallest room, the one without windows, they've removed all of the electrical outlets."

"Because –?" Becky dropped her Berkeley Number Seven brush into a pot of turpentine.

"They have to use candles in the room. They can't use artificial light. Artificial light might affect the prophecies of their seer stone."

Becky's voice went cold. "Psychics."

"You don't like fortune-tellers?" Uncertainty crept into Susannah's voice. "It's not what you think. They don't charge anything. They wouldn't even take my tip."

"Do *not* tell me you went up those stairs."

"It's only a game."

"It's a wicked game," Becky told her. "Let me finish cleaning up. I'll put the tea kettle on to heat and we can talk."

* * *

Seated at the kitchen table, she stirred a packet of artificial sweetener into her cup of green tea. "It was years and years ago," Becky said. "Rick and I were fairly new to this area. We'd emptied our bank account to buy our first place together. This house."

"I've always liked your house." Holding the tea cup in front of her mouth, Susannah surveyed the cream-colored walls around her. "It's so homey."

"We wanted a place to raise our baby, our little Kristin. We had so many plans. There was just so much... so much we planned to do."

116

Funny how the memory of it still hurts, she thought. *Nearly two decades later and talking about what-should-have-been still carries the ache of a fresh wound.*

People say the loss of a loved one becomes easier over time. That's partly true but only partly.

The loss never fully goes away.

"It was the middle of the week, for some reason we were both home, and I wanted to get out," she said. "There was no real reason for it. The house needed all kinds of repairs, the yard was a mess. There were a hundred chores waiting to be done."

"There are always a hundred chores to be done," Susannah said, blowing a cooling breath over the edge of her teacup.

"I'll never forget it. It was such a beautiful spring day. Rick would have been happy to putter around the place but I wanted to get out. So out we went."

* * *

The stroller's wheels clicked as they rolled over the divisions in the sidewalk. Ahead of them, the Downtown District was almost empty of pedestrians.

Becky was surprised at how quickly she'd grown to accept Winterhaven's vacant parking spaces and open sidewalks. She was enjoying life away from the big city. With her baby asleep in the stroller and her husband beside her, she felt content.

"Have you been watching?" Rick asked.

"Watching what?"

"How many people we've passed," he said. "We're in the heart of downtown and we've passed three other

117

people. Three. Not one of them carrying a shopping bag. The store lights are on, the doors are open, and the streets are practically empty. Why isn't the mayor doing something about this?"

"There's the Pumpkin Festival in October."

"So, for those two weeks, we get a few tourists in town. Two weeks! If it wasn't for Christmas and the Pumpkin Festival, every merchant in town would go bankrupt. It's not enough."

"The city's building a new mall. That might help."

"Could be."

"You wouldn't like all those tourists, anyway. Filling the stores, crowding the driving lanes. It drives you nuts."

"Don't go using logic on me," Rick told her. "I'll gripe and complain all I want, logic be damned. A good wife understands this. A good wife encourages her husband to spout the nonsense of his choice. A good wife simply nods her head and says, 'Yes, dear'."

"Yes, dear."

Rick leaned over and kissed her. Breaking off the kiss, his eyes widened. "Would you look at that?"

The front door of the Antiques Hut had a *We're Open* sign suctioned to the glass above its door handle. Below the faded letters of the store's name, a white placard was mounted: UNDER NEW MANAGEMENT.

"I thought they were out of business."

"It's been closed since we moved here." Rick rocked the stroller on its front wheels and backed into the doorway. "Let's go inside."

"No, you don't, mister. This isn't a shopping expedition."

"Did I say I wanted to buy anything?" He pushed open the door, causing a tiny brass bell to tinkle from its perch inside the building. "Let's just see what they've got."

"Oh, joy. We're teaching our baby how to be a looky-loo."

Rick continued ahead, somehow squeezing the stroller through the shop's narrow center aisle. Following after him, Becky quickly got a sense of this new business.

Different management? If so, it's the only thing new about this place.

Overhead lights threw a harsh fluorescent glow onto the shelves and tables below, revealing an inventory that appeared to have filled this space for years. A light film of dust seemed to cover everything. Around her, Becky saw old magazines, old knick knacks, old furniture and old toys.

Please don't find a vintage train set, she pleaded with Rick silently. *Nothing by Lionel or Ives or American Flyer, nothing you'll fall in love with. As much as you like your collection, we just can't afford another splurge right now.*

If Rick was swayed by her mental plea, he made no sign of it. He pushed the stroller ahead slowly, offering a mild interest in the goods around him.

She let her attention drift to a table filled with toys. A chinless, brown-faced figure sat in a red and green car with white wheels. Reaching for the string tied beneath the brim of the driver's black hat, she flipped over its price tag.

It read, *Andy Gump $95.*

119

A low whistle escaped her lips. Behind her, the brass bell jingled at the store's entrance.

"Oh, I'm so sorry," said a woman as she entered. "Customers. I was just next door. I didn't see you come in."

"That's okay."

Moving so quietly she might have been floating, the woman approached her. Seeing the rectangular tag in Becky's hand, she said, "All prices are negotiable."

Becky dropped her hand from the toy. "Just looking."

"Of course."

The woman smiled a distracted smile. She appeared to be about the same age as Becky but her tiny frame gave her an appearance of youth that her manner belied.

God, I'm a whale, Becky thought. *A little post-baby fat is natural but I'll never be as thin as this store clerk.*

If she was any skinnier, I'd see right through her.

Rick had journeyed to the back of the store, near a curtained area in the building's rear corner. The stroller sat in front of him. Miraculously, Kristin was still asleep.

Her husband held a silver metal train engine. He turned it over, examining the bottom of the toy.

Becky quickly navigated her way down the aisle. "Things are awfully expensive here," she said in a low voice.

"It's not discount store prices, that's for sure." He set the train engine on its table stand. "Nothing special, really."

"So why aren't we leaving?"

"Aren't you curious where they keep the good stuff?" he asked. "There's a room behind the curtain. I can smell incense burning."

"We can't, for a second, afford the cheapest of this junk. Why would I want to see the 'good stuff'?"

Rick raised an arm into the air. "Miss!"

The sales clerk swiveled in their direction. Slowly, she approached them, showing little enthusiasm for the task.

She knows we can't afford any of her goods. Even though it was true, Becky felt offended.

"What's your name?" Rick asked the clerk.

"Lenore Rice."

"What's behind the curtain, Lenore?"

The clerk's body stiffened. She narrowed her eyes, her vacant expression disappearing.

At first, Becky thought something was wrong. Then she realized: *The sales clerk is angry.* It was true. Her body was rigid, her small hands nearly curled into fists.

Becky said, "Do you mind if we call you 'Lenore'?"

After a moment, the woman's lips parted. "I much prefer my full name."

Becky and Rick shared a quick look. As if responding to the tension in the room, Kristin stirred inside her stroller. Becky picked her up, sweeping the pink blanket around her before it could trail to the floor.

Holding the baby to her chest, Becky rubbed her palm soothingly on her infant's cheek. Kristin nestled into her mother's arms, closing her eyes.

Lenore Rice viewed the child as if she'd found an unexpected treat.

121

"Well, then, Lenore Rice," Rick said, amused. "The full name it is, then. Mind answering my question?"

"Kristin's getting restless," Becky lied. "Let's go."

"In a minute."

Lenore Rice remained focused on the baby. Feeling uncomfortable under her gaze, Becky used her body to shield Kristin from the other woman. "I'll be outside."

Leaving, she heard Lenore Rice say to her husband, "Why don't I show you what's on the other side of the curtain?"

* * *

"So?" Susannah rested the base of her empty tea cup on the tabletop. "What was on the other side?"

"I think you know."

"A fortune-teller."

"Psychic, fortune-teller, they're all the same thing," Becky said. "Rick went into the back area and there she was. She apparently remained in her room all day, a spider in the darkness, waiting for –" *The next sucker*, she thought, before amending, "– a customer to come along. Rick said she had all the paraphernalia."

"Such as?"

"Tarot cards, tea leaves, those kinds of things. Probably had a crystal ball tucked in there somewhere, too. She was dressed like a gypsy, too. Might even have been a gypsy, for all I know."

"Did he get a reading?"

"It cost us seven dollars."

"Seven dollars isn't so much."

"It was seven dollars we couldn't afford," Becky said. "That little fee caused the owner of the store some trouble later on. Apparently, one of their customers didn't like what he'd been told and he went to the police. It seems, if a fortune-teller charges to give a reading, they have to have a business license. And this county doesn't give business licenses to psychics."

"Well, my reading at the café was different. No charge, remember?"

"Why do they do it, then?"

"For fun. An amusement for their customers." On Becky's expression, she added, "That's what they said."

"Was it fun? Did they give you the winning lottery numbers?"

"These old bones aren't climbing those stairs for some lottery numbers," Susannah said. "I wanted to know about romance."

"George Newton?"

"Maybe George, if he ever glances up from his drafting tools and notices I'm still alive. Maybe somebody else."

"So? Are you going to be lucky in love?"

"She said she didn't see anyone."

"She couldn't fake it?" Becky asked, surprised.

"I wish she had. Instead, she told me about my health. She said I'd never hurt like my abuela."

"That's because you told her about your grandmother's arthritis."

"Not a word, I swear," Susannah said. "'The next five years of your life are going to be perfect,' she told me."

"After that?"

123

"That's all she'd say. Five healthy, happy years. Right now, I'll take it. Besides, a short-term prophecy is good for repeat business. If nothing else, she knows I'll be back sooner or later."

"Believe what you want," Becky sipped at her tea. It had grown cold. "All I know is, the woman at the antiques store lied to Rick. She told him we'd never be rich but we'd never be poor. Our future together was going to be so bright, so wonderful."

Suddenly, tears filled her eyes. "Three days later, he was dead."

Susannah reached over to pat her hand. "Oh, honey. God knows –"

"Don't talk to me about God. No just God would kill a man as good as my husband."

They looked up at the sound of footsteps. Kristin paused in the kitchen's doorway, a nearly-empty bowl of popcorn in her hand.

"Kristin?" Becky said.

Gazing fixedly at their family friend, Kristin shook, a tremor running down her body. The bowl spilled from her hand. It struck the linoleum, cracking apart loudly as it threw popcorn kernels into the air and across the kitchen floor.

The noise seemed to awaken her. "I'm..." she said. "I don't – sorry. Clumsy." She blinked down at the broken bowl and its contents. "I'll get the broom."

Susannah considered the debris littering the floor. Hopefully, she said, "You have popcorn?"

Chapter Twenty

Kristin swept the shards of the broken bowl into a dustpan.

One of Mom's favorite bowls, she thought. *She's had it since I was a baby. I've been eating popcorn out of it ever since I can remember.*

Serves her right, sneaking into my bedroom.

Lifted from the ground, the mouth of the dustpan slapped closed.

No, she told herself, *no, it doesn't. She probably had her reasons. It started to rain and she checked my window or I cried out in my sleep or something.*

Some solid, Mom-type reason. Nothing sinister.

What's the matter with me?

She poured the pieces into the trash, watching the bowl's fragmented red-and-white flowers slide from the dustpan like so many puzzle pieces.

Ungood, she told herself. *Something in Winterhaven is majorly ungood.*

First, there were the glass people. Now, there's something wrong with Susannah.

In front of her, their family friend remained at the kitchen table, drinking a fresh cup of tea. Somebody didn't sit braless in their favorite red sweater, talking and laughing and drinking Sencha green tea, if something was wrong.

But Kristin knew something was wrong, nonetheless.

125

Walking into the kitchen, she hadn't been thinking about Susannah or anyone else. She'd been thinking about cars.

There was the kind of car she wanted – small, four-door, and blue, preferably electric but at least offering decent gas mileage – versus whatever embarrassment she could realistically hope to own. Expecting the kitchen to be empty, she was surprised to see anyone, much less Susannah –

– and, at the sight of her, everything went white. Her vision gone, Kristin stopped in place. When she did, the smell of plastic pressed upon her, so strong she almost gagged. A rasping sound split the air around her, shocking her, and sending the popcorn bowl dropping to the ground.

As quickly as the sound faded, her sight returned. "Sorry. Clumsy." She left to find the hand broom and dustpan, the odor of plastic still lingering in the air.

First her dream and, now, this? Susannah was in danger. Kristin needed to find out why and how. Someway, she was going to have to do something about it.

"Tomorrow, maybe," she told the trash can at her feet.

"Tomorrow, what, hon?" her mother asked.

Oh, good, now I'm talking out loud.

"Tomorrow, I'm going for lunch at Piotrowski's Café."

* * *

Cranking the steering wheel, Hawkins said, "There's a parking spot in front of the restaurant."

Kristin said, "It's a café, not a restaurant."

126

"There's a difference?"

"A café serves fine food. A restaurant serves those Sloppy Joes."

Hawkins stuck his tongue out at her.

"That was a little random," Kristin said.

"You, too," he said. "I'm taking the front spot."

"You are not." Seated behind them, Liz slouched a little lower. "Park at the side of the building. Out of sight."

"You're ashamed to be seen in my car?"

"With all of my heart, yes," she replied.

Kristin said, "I'm not ashamed of your car."

"Thank you."

"I think it's cute, all black and dented and rusted. I like how it puffs smoke whenever you start its engine."

"Look...."

"I have looked," Liz joined in. "I looked again this morning. I'm more embarrassed than ever."

A sour expression on his face, Hawkins spun the steering wheel. "It's a better car than the one you're driving."

"It is only because I'm not driving anything that you are correct."

He guided the vehicle into the dirt lot beside the café. "Next time, you both walk."

"Bless you." Pushing her door open, Liz stepped outside. "This gravel isn't going to do my Corso Como sandals any good."

"I weep to hear of your suffering," Kristin said.

"This is your treat?" Hawkins asked her.

"I said it was."

"There has to be a catch."

Liz caught at Kristin's sleeve. "Be honest."

127

The solemnity of her tone caught Kristin by surprise. She looked at her friend with concern.

"Am I dying?" Liz asked.

Hawkins said, "That could be the explanation." On Kristin's expression, he added, "Kidding."

"I'm not cheap."

"Never said you were."

Liz said, "What you are is unemployed."

"No paycheck, no money. Forced to live off your meager life's savings."

"Vis-à-vis, broke."

"You want lunch or not?" Kristin asked.

"Food is a welcome thing."

"We are not ungrateful," Liz added, "only the tiniest bit suspicious."

Liz wasn't the only one uneasy about their afternoon excursion. As Kristin mounted the steps of the porch, the rail-thin ghost woman she'd seen before – *Alice Poe, that's her name* – stepped from the entrance. When she saw her newest customers, she nearly fell over herself, trying to return inside.

Hawkins said, "There's the famous Piotrowski customer service everyone raves about."

Almost immediately, another woman came through the door. Every bit as translucent as Alice Poe, she seemed not nearly as nervous at meeting them.

In fact, she didn't appear nervous at all.

"Welcome to my café," she said. "My name is Mrs. Norton."

* * *

Entering the building, Kristin felt as if time had stood still.

Piotrowski's Café was reborn. Its wall decorations were unchanged and, curiously enough, they'd been placed in nearly the same locations as the originals. The furniture had reappeared from storage, white linens draping down the sides of the tables, and even the menus appeared to have survived the transition in ownership. It was as if Martin Piotrowski had hoarded every bit of his failed business, keeping it intact in the hope it might someday be reborn.

If this was his ambition, it had been realized. From the silverware with the stylized '*P*' on its stems to the Art Deco numberless clock hanging over the cash register, this version of the café was a close copy of the original.

Glancing at the customers in the room, Kristin saw some of the same regulars who populated the place in its heyday. With the lunch rush over and only five tables occupied, even the first café's impending failure had seemingly been duplicated.

There's one big difference, she thought. *There's no Martin, no Chandra, no me. No sign of Linda Sullivan, the weekday waitress, either.*

The friendly faces of my former co-workers have been replaced by the ghost people. The ghost peoples' faces aren't friendly at all.

Four crystal faces watched her as she trailed behind Mrs. Norton. The group huddled together in a tight knot at the rear of the restaurant, not far from the doorway leading into the kitchen.

129

She didn't know what to make of it. Try as she might, she couldn't read these people – if anyone so empty of flesh could even be called a person.

The tall, unpleasant Mr. Locke was at the front of the group, an odd expression on his face. Alice Poe held onto his arm, as frightened as a doe. Beside her, a chef's smock knotted around his waist, was Mr. Brass.

An old woman lingered by the kitchen door. Her features were softer than the others, her skin molded from colorless plastic instead of crystal. Hunched forward, her twisted left hand clutched the head of a wooden cane. Inside the folds of her face, a pair of dull gray eyes regarded Kristin warily.

"Miss Sweet, aren't you needed in your room?" Mrs. Norton asked.

The old woman shrank back as if she'd been rebuked. Dragging a leg behind her, the crone left.

"Mr. Brass, Mr. Locke?"

Mr. Brass dipped his head obediently. When Mr. Locke responded too slowly, the bigger man gripped the apron over his chest and tugged it sharply. Anger flashed across the thinner man's face but he moved forward. Picking up a plastic tray, he started collecting dirty dishes.

From somewhere in the restaurant, Kristin heard a *thump... thump... thump* sound. At first, she couldn't place it. Then she realized it was the sound of rubber striking wood. Miss Sweet was dragging herself up the interior stairway, her cane striking each step as she climbed higher.

Without waiting for her employer to speak, Alice Poe collected three menus and brought them to the corner table. Mrs. Norton rested a hand on the table's linen, smoothing a wrinkle which didn't exist. "Can I start you with an appetizer?"

Liz scooted her chair forward. "Dare we?"

Kristin shot her a look.

"We dare not," Hawkins said. "Water all around, thanks."

Alice Poe darted forward with a pitcher. She filled their glasses, a slight tremor in her hand. When the water had been poured, Mrs. Norton touched the server's arm to lightly draw her attention.

Kristin lifted her menu. She peeked over its top edge, her eyes following the pair as they walked off.

Hawkins asked Liz, "Any word on Mouser?"

"Not yet." She opened her menu. "Stupid cat."

"You know, Miss Boots is missing, too."

"Your cat's always missing," Liz told him. "Little slut."

Kristin let her gaze drop to the menu selections. The first inside page offered appetizers. On the back, there was a page listing the café's drinks and desserts. The other pages consisted of entrees and specials.

"Just like before," she said.

"Almost exactly like before," Hawkins agreed. "But 'before' was excellent."

"What I meant was, there's lots and lots of beef."

Liz released a huge sigh. "Not the vegetarian thing again."

"It's not 'again'. I've been a vegetarian for nearly four years."

Hawkins scanned the page in front of him. "Didn't they use to serve tilapia?"

"Fish still count!"

131

"Kristin, listen to me," Liz said earnestly. "Woman doesn't live on ferns and berries alone. It's not natural."

Mrs. Norton returned to their table. "Is there a problem?"

"Not as far as I'm concerned," Hawkins said.

"It's our beloved Saint Kristin of Winterhaven," Liz told her. "She eateth not of the flesh of the beast."

Kristin buried her face into the menu.

"Kristin?" Mrs. Norton asked. "Would you be Kristin Faraday?"

"That's our girl." Hawkins pointed to a line item on the menu. "They have side salads."

Mrs. Norton folded her hands around the order pad. Suspended in nothingness, her green eyes remained on Kristin's face.

"Martin told me about you," she said. "He mentioned you were special. A very special girl."

"Not really."

"He also said you needed a job."

Liz lifted her chin, studying the older woman. Mrs. Norton brought one of her hands from the order pad. Tucked between two fingers, she held a white business card. When Kristin made no effort to take the card, she laid it on their table.

Liz scooped it up. "Ashfork Imports and Oddities."

"Some friends of mine run the business," Mrs. Norton said. "It's quite high end."

"I don't know anything about imports," Kristin said softly.

"They're willing to train the right person. They're trying to find someone they can trust. Someone they can train to be an executive assistant."

132

"I don't know." Kristin felt a sharp stab of pain as Liz kicked her from under the table. Reluctantly, she took the card from her friend's hand. "It's over a hundred miles from here."

"Not too far for someone with ambition."

She let her eyes run over the embossed lavender printing. "There's no telephone number."

"They deal with an exclusive clientele. Monied people. They wouldn't dare leave their unlisted number on a card." She leaned closer still. "I'm certain you understand."

"*I* understand," Liz said. She gave Kristin a sharp look: *What's wrong with you?*

Holding the card, Kristin thought: *It's not me, Liz, it really isn't.*

This kindly middle-aged woman, the one smiling down at us? For me, her teeth aren't white. They're see-through rectangles. Inside her mouth, hidden behind her smile, is a barely visible tongue. Behind that, there's a blur at the center of her throat.

Something's moving *in there.*

"Mrs. Norton?" Alice Poe edged closer to the restaurant owner. She brought her mouth to the other woman's ear, whispering to her.

"Did he?" A hint of unhappiness touched Mrs. Norton's reply. "I'll take care of it in a moment."

Alice Poe dipped her head, a worried expression on her face.

Taking the business card, Mrs. Norton unclicked a pen and wrote across the card's face. "Let me give you the telephone number."

133

"Why?" Kristin asked. "Why are you doing this for me?"

"Martin recommended you. Good help really is hard to find."

"But you don't even know me." She flinched as her ankle suffered from another of Liz's kicks.

"It's a fantastic opportunity," the café's owner said. "You'd like that, wouldn't you? An exciting job that pays well?"

"I'm definitely interested," Liz said.

Mrs. Norton returned the business card to the tabletop. Written in red ink, the unlisted phone number ran along the bottom of the white rectangle.

"There's a little apartment on the premises, directly above the shop," she said. "For the right person, I doubt they'd even charge rent. Think about it. You could stay right there in Ashfork."

Hawkins lowered his menu to see what Kristin would say.

"Promise you'll call," Mrs. Norton said. "Please."

"I –" Kristin forced the words out. "All right, I promise."

Schhhct! The familiar stab of pain burned her face. Her mouth disappeared behind its mask.

Mrs. Norton's lips curled at the edges.

She can tell! She knows I'm lying!

"Never mind." Lifting the card, Mrs. Norton tore it in half. "Perhaps it's not what you really want, after all."

"No," the word was faint and blurred to Kristin's ears, "not really."

Schhhct! Her mouth returned to her.

134

"Alice Poe will be with you shortly," Mrs. Norton said pleasantly. "The tilapia is excellent. You might want to avoid the salads, though. The greens are a little bit off."

She left for the cash register. Quickly, Kristin raised her cell phone and took a picture of her.

Hawkins leaned over to see the phone's screen. "A fifty-year old woman in the middle of a restaurant. Great pic. You've gotta post that on your Facebook page."

Liz said, "You and I have to talk, girl. Are you nuts?" Her face changed, stricken at her choice of words. "I mean –"

"I know what you meant, Lizzer. It's okay." She surveyed the room. Mrs. Norton was talking softly and urgently to an unhappy Mr. Locke. Alice Poe fluttered behind them, listening while pretending not to do so.

Kristin dropped the menu to the table. "When the waitress comes back, find out if the pea soup has ham in it."

"You want something else to drink?"

"Diet cola."

Hawkins said, "Live a little. Try something without carbonation."

"Diet cola." She grabbed her purse. "I've got to use the little girl's room."

"It's all that diet cola."

`Liz said. "I'll go, too."

"Not this time," Kristin said, her voice low but forceful.

Liz dropped into her seat. "Whoa. Somebody seriously needs her private time."

135

Kristin walked toward the *Restrooms* sign on the far wall. Entering the corridor leading to the bathrooms, she turned toward a small alcove.

A closed door blocked her progress. The sign on the door read: STAFF ONLY   ALARM WILL SOUND!

Since when? she wondered.

"The alarm doesn't work," Piotrowski told her on her first day on the job. "The sign, that's what works. Nobody comes through here, anyway. Why would they? To go into the kitchen, be chased out by the cook?"

She hoped Mrs. Norton shared Martin's philosophy on alarm repair. Tentatively, she pushed the door open. The alarm remained silent as she entered the kitchen.

Silver preparation tables and service counters gleamed up at her. On one of the large commercial stoves, an aluminum stock pot roiled with boiling water. Beside the pot, a stainless-steel double boiler puffed softly, red blisters of tomato sauce breaking and reforming as they heated. From one of the ovens, she smelled the odor of baked cinnamon.

There was a place for everything and everything was in its place. Kristin was impressed. Each of the utensils hung from a post, arranged in order of size. All of the unused cookware was stored and there wasn't a scrap of food on the prep table. Martin Piotrowski, at his tidiest, couldn't have produced such a spotless kitchen.

What did it mean?

Probably nothing, she conceded.

In the midst of weirdness, an effort toward good sanitation shouldn't have left her uneasy. But it somehow did, a little.

136

Directly to her left were the wooden stairs leading to the building's second level. Upstairs, someone murmured soothingly.

This first voice was immediately answered by a second, louder voice. "I don't care about health issues. You're a fortune-teller. Tell me what I want to know. Tell me about my investments."

It sounded like Al Gerhardt's voice. But what was her old high school biology teacher doing on the upper floor?

Then: *Did he say fortune-teller? There's a fortune-teller here?*

From above, she heard *murmur, murmur, murmur* in response.

Placing a foot on the stairway's first step, Kristin heard the wood creak softly in protest. Resting her hand on the banister, she closed her eyes.

Taking a deep breath to steady herself, she told herself, "It's now or never."

"What say, 'never'?" a deep voice asked.

She opened her eyes as a huge meat cleaver crashed down in front of her. Splintered wood flew into the air. Jumping back, Kristin struck the side wall and fell, pieces of banister spraying around her.

Mr. Brass wrapped and rewrapped his thick glass fingers around the handle of the cleaver. "This kitchen is for employees only. Didn't you see the sign?"

Footsteps thudded loudly from overhead. Wearing a button-up shirt and an unknotted tie, Al Gerhardt leaned over the second story's half-wall. "What was *that?*"

"A little misunderstanding," Mr. Brass said. "It won't happen again."

Her cane thumping in front of her, Miss Sweet peered over the half-wall. She was dressed in a flowing skirt and a black blouse, with colorful scarves draping down her neck. Gerhardt threw a last puzzled look at the couple below before being led away by the fortune-teller.

Kristin climbed to her feet. "I'm going."

Mr. Brass locked his fingers over the rounded head of the stairway's first post, his arm blocking her path. In his other hand, he raised his meat cleaver.

"I'll scream," she said.

Keeping his hand on the post, he brought his other arm down sharply. The blade whistled as it fell, its sharp edge striking the thick hand on the post. The cook grunted as the cleaver struck home.

From the upstairs room, Al Gerhardt cried out, "What was *that?*"

Mr. Brass raised his hand to show it to her. He wiggled his fingers. Below the fingers, where the blade had struck, there was a spider web of cracks.

"Hurts like a son-of-a-bitch," he said, "but the marks will fade in a day or two. Want to see what happens when I try it on you?"

She put her hand against the apron over his chest. Ghost or not, he was solid. She pushed harder. The jacket went flat beneath her fingers, as if she'd pressed against brick or metal instead of flesh.

Finally, Mr. Brass allowed her to slide past. Moving quickly, she went out of the kitchen.

Hawkins and Liz looked up at her.

"We're going," Kristin said.

"I knew it." Hawkins lowered his water glass. "This is exactly what happened at IHOP last summer."

They were at the exit when a voice called out: "Kristin! Kristin Faraday!"

She turned. Waiting for a table, Susannah Guitierrez waved at her.

"Let's go," Liz said. "My reputation has suffered enough."

Kristin left hurriedly, the smell of plastic filling the air behind her.

Chapter Twenty-One

Cross-legged, she sat upon the wooden floor. Beneath her, somewhere inside the building's first level, she heard noises. The noises were soon followed by a sound of voices, both female.

Miss Sweet sighed.

Her thumb rolled against the flint wheel of a butane lighter, sending a flame from its barrel. Moving the rectangular lighter over the table in front of her, she touched its fire to the wicks of three candles. When all had caught flame, she rose and went to her closet.

She would dress as a gypsy, that was a given. Mrs. Norton insisted upon it. Not that this was anything like real gypsy garb. If she'd dressed like a real gypsy, wearing slacks and a JCPenney's' blouse, her patrons wouldn't have been impressed. They'd have questioned whether she could read the future.

People are so stupid, she thought. *Was I ever so foolish?*

Once upon a time, perhaps. When I was young and this body was still foreign to me. When I was my hungriest.

It was then I agreed to serve Mrs. Norton.

She shrugged the gown over her head, letting its coarse linen scratch over her breasts and belly as its hem tumbled to the floor. Reaching for the closet's upper shelf, she found an assortment of scarves to complete her outfit.

From the landing below, Mrs. Norton said, "Up the stairs, it's the first room on your left. Miss Sweet is waiting for you."

"It's so dark," a voice replied.

"Miss Sweet likes the dark."

Oh, yes, Miss Sweet acknowledged, *that much is true. I love the dark and the secrets it hides. I love the anonymity it offers.*

The only thing I love more is the feeding.

Grasping the sides of an old cigar box, she took it from the shelf. The box itself was a worthless thing, its wood scarred from age and ill-use. Lines were cut through the original manufacturer's name, leaving only a single word – TUCKETT – still legible.

Even the most hard-pressed thief would ignore this sad, worn receptacle. It was no one's idea of a collector's item.

She raised the lid gingerly, not wanting to break its remaining hinge. Inside the box, wrapped inside a satin cloth, was the blackest stone she'd ever seen. This miracle, this wonder, nearly filled the interior space.

Sliding her fingers under the stone, she lifted it up. At this moment, the rock was mute and blind. But given a taste of life, that would change.

She placed it between the burning candles. As perfect as a star, the seer stone shone with the reflected light of the flames floating above it. Miss Sweet blessed the day it had called to her.

She didn't know why she was chosen. The others were envious, she knew, but there was nothing they could do about it. They didn't have the gift. For all of her years, for all of her abilities, not even Mrs. Norton could bring the seer stone to life. She couldn't make it tell her the one thing she most needed to know: *Who has five years to give us?*

Miss Sweet opened a bronze pillbox. Removing a straight pin from its velvet center, she dragged the pin's tip across the floor.

She hoped the sharpened end would collect a bit of bacteria, some tiny harbinger of disease. She liked the thought of infection finding the needle's tip and waiting to be shared with the guest coming up the stairs.

In her years with the seer stone, a fouled pin had spoiled only one potential victim. Only one. She kept this knowledge to herself; oh, yes, this secret was hers and hers alone. There would be punishment if Mrs. Norton ever discovered her little game.

But she never would, would she? She didn't have the second sight.

She set the pin on the table in front of her, closing the pillbox as her patron appeared in the doorway.

"Are you Miss Sweet?"

"Welcome." She gestured for the woman to sit at the opposite end of the table. "Tell me your name."

"Shouldn't you know that already?" She gave a nervous laugh. "I'm Mary Ellen Stark."

She was nicely dressed, this Mary Ellen Stark, an expensive purse dangling from her shoulder. Despite the wedding ring on her right hand, there was an air of loneliness about her.

"Have you been doing this for very long?" Mary Ellen asked, sinking to the floor.

Miss Sweet pulled the straight pin between her thumb and index finger. "That's not what you've come to ask."

"I... guess not."

She waited.

"I want to know about my children," Mary Ellen said.

"Please. The truth."

"That is the truth."

"Later, you may want to know about your children," Miss Sweet said. "Some other time, perhaps, we'll enjoy such a discussion. Not this evening. Tonight, you want to know about yourself. On the first visit, your kind wants to know about their future, not the future of others."

"My kind?" Under the candles' yellow light, Mary Ellen frowned.

Miss Sweet took her hand, and said, soothingly, "It's only natural."

"I want to know about Jackson," Mary Ellen said. "Jackson Lawrence. Does he still care about me?"

Miss Sweet tightened her fingers over the woman's hand. Twisting her wrist, she stabbed the stickpin into the ball of her client's thumb.

"Owww!" Instinctively, Mary Ellen tried to yank away from her.

Miss Sweet kept the hand imprisoned. "You want to know about love? In all of the hand, only the Mount of Venus holds those answers."

She brought the woman's hand closer as a bubble of blood rolled from the skin's surface. The crimson drop melted onto the seer stone, flattening as it hit the obsidian surface.

"That's *blood*," Mary Ellen said. "My blood on your... your rock."

"Did you think the future came without a price?"

"I hope the pin was sterile!"

"Tell me to stop and I will. Tell me to reach into your future and I'll do that, instead."

"It's done now." Mary Ellen stuck her injured thumb inside her mouth. "Do it. Do… whatever."

Miss Sweet put an index finger at each side of the seer stone's apex. She rested her thumbs at opposite ends of its base. "You wanted to know about Jackson Lawrence."

Dropping the injured hand from her mouth, Mary Ellen peered into the rock.

They all gazed at the stone, those who came to her. What did they hope to see? Did they think the stone would talk to them?

How could it? They were already blind to the world around them. What made them think they could see magicks?

Held in Miss Sweet's fingers, the rock opened itself to her. Across its face, dots of color appeared. Shimmering, the dots spun, faster and faster, becoming an unrecognizable swirl.

Inside the swirl, an image formed. It was a middle-aged man of average height, his body starting to soften. He sat alone in his house, the light of a television set shining onto him and his overstuffed chair.

Miss Sweet said, "He waits in solitude. He has no one." The swirl swept over him, a wave of red. "His heart aches."

"For who? I mean, is there someone he wants? Someone he needs?"

Miss Sweet gave thought to her question and the answer appeared. A silver-haired woman stood inside a small fenced yard. A hedge trimmer in hand, she shaped the branches of a small green bush.

The woman was not Mary Ellen Stark.

"There is," Miss Sweet said. The view of the woman wavered before her then froze. It became a still picture, its color disappearing. Like a picture, it curled at the edges then blackened, crumbled, and disappeared. "She's gone."

"Gone?"

"She died."

Mary Ellen's eyes brightened. "Then there's a chance –?"

Miss Sweet shook her head. "I don't see you with him."

"Jack has always had a thing for me. Even before he met Diana."

"All I can offer is the truth."

"What you *say* is the truth!"

Someone came up the stairway, taking the stairs with a heavy step. Raising her eyes, Miss Sweet gazed past Mary Ellen and into the hallway.

No one was there.

Undoubtedly, the candlelight had let the others know she was at work. Whoever this new visitor was, they were staying out of sight. Eavesdropping on her words.

Listening for whatever she might say next to her new client.

145

Which meant it had to be Mr. Locke. If Alice Poe was true to form, she was standing next to him, her fingers locked in his.

Not because she wished to know of this woman's future. Only because she was oblivious to her own.

"Enough of what isn't to be," Miss Sweet said. "Instead, let me consider the life you have yet to live."

Inside the stone, the dots turned to mist. Through the mist, Mary Ellen slept on her bed. A new vision of Mary Ellen formed, still sleeping, but slightly thinner.

Again –

Again –

Again, she appeared. Growing older with each new appearance. "You have five years ahead of you."

"Only five?"

"The next five years is all I'm given. All I'm allowed to see." The mist blew across the center of the stone. Inside, Mary Ellen held a letter, weeping onto the page in front of her.

"The first year will be marred by sorrow."

Her sentence stirred the lurkers in the hallway. The corridor creaked unhappily as Mr. Locke went down the hall. Alice Poe followed after him, mewing words of weak comfort.

Unseen winds shifted inside the seer stone, sending a cloud of dots swirling around the woman inside. When Miss Sweet saw Mary Ellen's image, she was on a hospital stretcher, her eyes closed as she was pushed forward.

"The second year is marred by disease."

The fog covered the vision of the woman. When it lifted, it showed her in the embrace of a gray-haired man.

146

The man was a stranger to Miss Sweet. Short and rotund, he wasn't Jackson Lawrence.

The tiny image of Mary Ellen beamed as the stranger leaned in to kiss her.

"In the third year, you'll find joy." She raised her hands from the stone.

"What kind of joy?"

"It's vague, uncertain." Her lips tingled, threatening to melt. Reluctantly, she said, "I saw a man, well-dressed, with short, gray hair. He was holding you."

"I don't know anyone like that."

"In three years, you will."

Clearly doubtful, Mary Ellen stood from the table. "What else?"

"Let some time pass and we can talk again."

"You talked about five years."

"That's what I seek for my clients. Five years of strength and good health. Five years of happiness. Five perfect years." Miss Sweet puffed at the flame of the closest candle. "Do you know how hard that is to find?"

Mary Ellen shifted the strap of her purse. "Are you really a gypsy?"

"I never said I was a gypsy."

"You're not?"

"My people came before the gypsies. Before the Travelers. Our people have ever been."

The second candle's light passed over the folds in her sour face. She blew on its wick and the candle vanished into darkness. With pride, Miss Sweet said, "We will ever be. We are the Unending."

Mary Ellen shivered, as if she felt a chill run down her spine. "I'd better go."

* * *

Tall and slim and perfect, he waited at her bedroom window. When she'd seen him the first time, his skin was the color of caramel. His hair was straight and black, his eyes warm and brown. The first time, he seemed more beautiful than one of the Gods.

Now, nearly empty, he still made her heart race. A translucent statue, he scowled at the street below them.

"There she goes," Mr. Locke said. "Flawed. Useless."

"You have to be patient."

"Because she says we have to be patient, right? It's the only reason, isn't it? We do as she tells us."

Yes, Alice Poe thought, *but there's wisdom in what Mrs. Norton says. It never hurts to be patient. Patience can feed our family. A rash act can send us all running.*

I'm so tired of running.

On the street, a car engine purred to life. Watching as its headlights illuminated an empty sidewalk, Mr. Locke said, "Miss Sweet wastes her time with these old ones. She should focus on the young. They have the years we need. Most of them have five times the years we need!"

"They have to be of age."

"You don't think I know?" Releasing the window curtain, he turned to her. "You've told me often enough. Everyone here treats me as if I'm fresh from the Void. It's been a year."

"Nearly a year."

"If we took the meat at seventeen years old, eighteen years old, we'd have more than enough for our needs. We could all feed tomorrow."

"There's too much turmoil at that age. Upheaval, uncertainty, change. Such things are hard on us. To avoid it, Miss Sweet would have to see a hundred –"

"Then bring her a hundred! There's no shortage of them!"

Not responding, Alice Poe knitted her fingers together.

Mr. Locke rubbed his hand across his eyes. "How many of their kind did she see this week?"

"Fifteen."

"To find one. One we can use."

"She'll find others."

"Not soon enough." He pushed her and she fell upon the bed frame's bare mattress. He towered over her. Even this depleted, he appeared so powerful. So ready to act.

She felt frightened.

She felt aroused.

"Did the Dark Ones give me this body," he said, sweeping his hands down his bare chest, "only to have me starve?"

He waited above her, posing. Alice Poe wanted him and she knew he sensed it. She knew, too, how little he wanted her.

It should have mattered and it did – but not enough. She'd never desired anyone more. "You'll feed. Just not yet."

Contempt filled his eyes. When he spoke, his words were so deep as to have come from the Void itself. "I'm *hunnnnnnnngry.*"

Chapter Twenty-Two

Mr. Locke's growl came to her from the adjoining room. His words were lost behind the walls but Mrs. Norton knew what he wanted. What they *all* wanted, even her.

Everything in due time.

She scratched a wooden match across the face of the ceramic table. The match flared to life, smelling pleasantly of phosphorus, and she touched its head to the wick of a squat, turquoise candle. A bead of flame caught hold, grew larger, and licked at the air beneath her hand.

At a push of her fingers, the bedroom door slid closed. Its latch caught so quietly she barely heard it.

Its walls painted gray, its only window painted over, the room was nearly as black as a tomb, with only the wavering finger of the candle's flame providing any light. In the middle of the room, barely visible in the gloom, was a large, raised platform. Invisible in the shadows, a black cabinet filled the chamber's furthest corner.

This was her space. The others knew they were not welcome here, especially during her time of worship. For safety's safe, she'd arranged for Miss Sweet to be occupied and given Alice Poe and Mr. Locke new chores.

While Alice Poe worked, Mr. Locke would hide himself away. Neither one would come to her door. She didn't concern herself with Mr. Brass. Unless she called him, he wouldn't dare interrupt her.

Years ago, shortly after he'd entered her service, he'd been punished for his curiosity. He never wanted to be punished again.

Tonight, she couldn't indulge in her usual communion. She wouldn't chant from the Book of Forgotten Lies; she wouldn't drink from the Cup of Misery; there would be no animal sacrifices. The canary she'd purchased would remain caged in the café's storage unit, trilling in terror.

Maybe I'll let it starve, she thought mildly.

This particular bird acted less stupidly than most of its kind. If she let it die, no one would notice. Besides, pet stores kept a flock of the yellow things. The clerks never questioned why she wanted a new one every seven days.

She'd always been comforted by her weekly rituals but dared not enjoy herself tonight. She had a question to ask her gods and an interruption at an inopportune time could have dire consequences for them all. It was best if she acted quickly.

Carrying the candle's silver holder to the cabinet, Mrs. Norton watched as the box's intricate carvings danced below the yellow light. When she rested the base of the holder on top of the container, the carvings hissed at her.

"Foul mood, my little *Wunderkammer*?"

The engraved images shifted and flowed, circling the candle holder and reaching for it. Trapped in ebony, they writhed unhappily, forming and reforming, but forever unable to escape their lacquered prison.

151

Grasping a pair of ivory handles, Mrs. Norton opened the cabinet doors. Pulling out the first of the container's four drawers, she considered the offerings there.

Not many left. I'll have to tell Mr. Brass.

Pinching a thin rectangle between her forefinger and thumb, she laid it onto the palm of her opposite hand. Soon, eight tiny strips had been collected. Two of the rectangles were nearly as dark as the box itself. Two were brown in color and the remaining four were in varying shades of peach.

All were marked with letters and a number, the symbols inked by her hand. Other than the markings upon them, there was nothing distinctive about the rectangles. Each piece was more common than a blister beetle, more fragile than paper. Each specimen had come from an individual donor but only one of these sections had been donated willingly.

At her command, Mr. Brass would walk the streets, seeking more of the wards, but even he had grown tired of the chore. It would be less challenging if people weren't so possessive about their skin.

She circled the room, placing each *telesma*. Soon, the walls, the doorway and the black window were locked. Only the ceiling remained unsealed and available as a portal to other dimensions.

From this point on, Mrs. Norton would have to suffer. At one time, she'd have gloried in the pain, stimulated by the heat of her discomfort. Now, there was only the knowledge of the danger ahead.

To her surprise, she felt a whisper of... *something*... drumming quietly inside of her. Was it fear?

If so, there was reason. Once released into the world, few of the Unending dared scratch at the Void's door. One errant note, one misplaced sound, and the wrong deity might answer. Summoned without cause, an angry god might choose to return a careless supplicant to the fold.

How long had it been since she was afraid? Decades?

Inside the cabinet's lowest, deepest drawer was her blade, wicked and cursed. She lifted the knife from its bed. Refusing to indulge herself in the luxury of hesitation, she clutched its handle tightly. The thousand tiny needles mounted on the hilt impaled her palm, biting into her.

Mrs. Norton gasped but held her voice. As the wires pierced her hand, there was a *swoosh* of sound. The candlelight vanished as air escaped from the room. The strips of skin brightened, each rectangle glowing, as the space around her lost its light. The dark blade in her hand turned white, its luminosity guiding her to the platform at the center of the room.

Sinking to the middle of the square, Mrs. Norton rested to her knees. She opened her mouth, screaming at last, knowing the vortex would capture the sound and swallow it.

Inside her throat, her hunger whirled, faster and faster, singing inside of her. It cried for attention, pleading for notice, begging, *begging* for Khagean the Guardian to hear its prayer.

Mrs. Norton's body shook, vibrating as she made her incantation. Extending her arm, she cut into it with the edge of the knife. The fine tip slipped beneath her crystalline skin, carving a trail of fire from her wrist to

153

the center of her forearm. Agony washed over her but her vocalization never wavered.

She dropped the blade, letting it fall beside her. Her arm wept, a single clear pearl splashing onto the knife.

Her body burning, her head bent, she felt the vortex start to slow. The platform trembled beneath her. Above her, the ceiling opened and was gone. She sensed rather than saw the emptiness erupting above her head.

One of the deities was manifest. Although it could never truly *be* in this reality, the Dark One was as close as a whisper, its presence brushing at the nape of her neck. She could feel its enormous power.

Inside herself, she heard his voice. ***Tell me.***

Khagean was the Guardian of the Void and he had come to her. Twice before, he had answered her call and, twice before, he had deigned to answer her questions. Consequently, all of her sacrifices were made in his name. When she triumphed, she thanked the Guardian in her prayers. When she failed, she cursed his enemies for her fate.

Ever his faithful servant, she dared take little for granted. She knew she must pose her question carefully, saying nothing of Kristin Faraday. Her Lord did not care about mortals.

Nor did she, the truth be told. It aggravated her that the girl, this insignificant *thing*, was somehow still alive. Alive and here, in Winterhaven, as if she was normal and whole.

What was wrong with her family? Even if they lacked the decency to rid the world of her, why weren't they shamed enough to flee with the pest, taking her to another city? Yet, here she remained... and she was curious about her betters.

Her very existence had brought Mrs. Norton to her knees. Alice Poe, Miss Sweet, Mr. Brass – they carried no obligation to the Other. If they choose to leave, they could.

Not that they'd survive for long without her.

Finally, she asked the one thing she needed to know: *May I leave this place?*

This is why you summoned me?

An irritated wind whipped around Mrs. Norton's body. She heard the silver candle holder fall from its perch, clattering to the ground.

You bother me with THIS?

Was the Guardian somehow unaware of her situation? It was possible, she supposed. His duty was to the Void. His interest in his followers was, at most times, superficial.

Mrs. Norton fought to clear her thoughts, keeping her secret to herself. It was for naught.

A new voice entered her: ***It's because of the girl.***

Ajanosek, the Protector of Newborns, carried no love for Mrs. Norton or her kind. The Protector was rarely cruel without reason but she could be vengeful.

You stole from her, Ajanosek chastised.

It was a trifle, Goddess, Mrs. Norton offered. *The tiniest of thefts. I meant no disrespect.*

A debt is owed.

The words twisted in Mrs. Norton's stomach, threatening to make her sick.

The girl must be given an opportunity to make her claim.

An opportunity? I understand, my Goddess. I obey, my Goddess.

But for how long? How much time must pass while she ponders her choices?

Above her head, the cosmos swirled.

What if the girl should leave this place? Mrs. Norton asked. *Or if she should choose to – to make a more permanent exit?*

Suddenly, the sensation of illness was gone. Mrs. Norton felt well and whole and, for the moment, not hungry.

Without words, Ajanosek had given her the answer. With his silence, Khagean had allowed the answer to stand.

The room fell into darkness, its ceiling in place again. The gods had returned to their dimension.

And, for now, Mrs. Norton would remain in Winterhaven.

Chapter Twenty-Three

His dead wife said, "Where have you been, Howard?"

What could he say that wouldn't anger her? Start with the truth, perhaps. "The doctor told me I needed more sleep, Eustacia. I only did what the doctor said."

"You're sleeping now."

"It's not the same," the Reverend Hawkins said. "When I see you at night, it haunts me throughout the day. Because... because I miss you so."

She smiled, torn flesh rising.

"You've been coming to me so often lately. Two or three times a week. I thought, with a little more rest, I'd be better company."

"Silly." She fluttered her remaining eye flirtatiously. "I like your company, no matter what. I want you with me always."

He knew she did. He used to want the same thing. "The medications help me sleep more soundly."

"Medications." The tone of her voice went flat. "You mean, drugs."

"Medicine. Prescribed medicine. Doctor Barnes –"

"Drugs are the gateway to Satan's playground," Eustacia interrupted. "How many times have you said that very thing from behind your lectern? How many times have you implored your congregation to *do the right thing*?"

157

"Not prescription drugs, darling."

"It's a fine line, Howard. A damned fine line."

Now she *was* angry. She never cursed unless she was angry.

She turned the shattered half of her body toward him, forcing him to confront the damage she'd suffered. "Does Gideon know?"

"It's none of Gideon's business."

"Has he seen you swallow your pills? Does he watch his father stagger about in a stupor?"

"No."

"Has he seen you stumbling about like a common drunk?"

"It's Ambien, love, that's all." He swallowed deeply. "One white tablet. The smallest dose."

"Well."

"I'm cautious when I take it. I never drive after. Never."

She softened, showing the undamaged portion of her face. "I only ask because I care."

"Of course." He reached out his hand, stroking the unbroken skin at the left side of her cheek.

"Do you remember the last time we talked?"

"You know I do." He wasn't sure he did, though. Sometimes, the dreams remained vivid for days. Lately, with Brenda in his life, some of those memories had started to blur.

"I told you there was evil in Winterhaven."

"Yes, you told me. I do remember."

"What are you doing about it?"

He tried to remember exactly what she'd said but nothing came to him. "Doing about the evil?"

"The unclean spirits." Her green eye fixed at him. "The ones who come to us from the mouth of the dragon and from the mouth of the beast."

Was she quoting scripture to him? Eustacia, who always liked being a preacher's wife but never quite found the time to open a Bible? "What do you want me to do?"

"Kristin Faraday."

"Kristin? Gideon's friend?" the Reverend asked. "What about her?"

His bedside alarm went off. His eyes came open. Eustacia was gone.

He breathed in slowly, calming himself.

Time to start the day.

* * *

His father was at the lectern, waiting for him. There was a bucket of soapy water at his feet and a large orange sponge in his right hand.

Hawkins' heart sank. "Lord, why hast thou forsaken me?"

"You know what I think about that kind of humor."

Yes, he surely did.

"Think before you speak, son," the Reverend continued. "The people in this community watch you. You're a role model for others."

Me, a role model? Hawkins thought. *Get real.*

How much of a role model could he be, when everybody knew his best friend wasn't a believer? She wouldn't come to his own church, no matter how often he asked. It bugged his father – it bugged him, too, truth be

159

told – and he knew people talked about it behind their backs.

Too bad. He loved Kristin.

Not in some perverse way. He didn't have those thoughts about her. He *did* have those thoughts about other women, he wasn't some religious 'bot free from lust in his heart, but Kristin was somehow absent from the graphic fantasies that intruded into his day.

He guessed most guys had similar needs. Did his father?

Once he'd have doubted it. Now....

"The windows?" Hawkins asked. "All of them?"

"From top to bottom."

"I cleaned the pews. Even the ones on the far-right side, the ones no one sits in."

"You did a good job of it, too. Ed couldn't have done any better."

"Can't the windows wait until he gets back?" His stone-faced father didn't bother with a reply. Hawkins let his shoulders slump forward. "Do you know how many windows we have in this place?"

"Since you ask, yes, I do. A man of the Lord knows everything about his particular house of worship."

"A preacher can't know everything about his church."

"Let us count the number," he told him. "Six windows in the nave, two on each side of the chancel, one at the apse, and two across from the altar. Thirteen windows."

"Okay, I get it," Hawkins said. "I need to pay more attention. But I did notice we have seven big stained-glass windows. I mean, *big*. When it comes to cleaning

160

something like that, a stained-glass window is like ten ordinary windows. That's seventy-six windows altogether."

Reverend Hawkins let the orange sponge drop into the bucket. "Good thing you got here early."

* * *

Mickey Mouse sat on the dashboard, his head bobbing on its coiled spring as the car cruised down the street. Mickey's bright happy face suggested he was in a much better mood than the frowning Liz Wheeler who waited at curbside.

"That's because Liz isn't a morning person," Kristin told Mickey as she directed the car to the side of the road.

Liz opened the passenger door. "I prayed your mother wouldn't let you borrow the car."

"She was good with it."

"Just my luck," Liz said, climbing inside. "I got up at dawn, just so we could drive over to Susannah's? You couldn't call her, instead?"

"I did call. Last night."

"And?"

"She's fine," Kristin admitted. "She wondered why I was on the phone, I think, but was too polite to mention it."

"But we're still going out to her place this morning. For some reason."

"Because I'm feeling gitchy about things."

"Well, why didn't you say so? Now I get it. You're gitchy." She folded her arms across her chest. "Do you

161

have any idea what time my alarm clock went off this morning?"

"Ten minutes ago?"

"That was your alarm clock, fashion disaster. Mine screeched at me over an hour ago." She surveyed her companion. "Girl, what's the matter with you? No make-up, no perfume, naked nails, and wearing shoes so out of style it would embarrass a hobo."

"A hobo?"

"What are you going to do if you meet the perfect man today?"

"Hope he likes someone with no make-up, no perfume, naked nails and hobo shoes."

"As if." Liz relaxed against the head rest. "At least we're not traveling in the Hawkmobile. This car is totally lacking in Cheetos smell."

"You'll notice the absence of mustard-stained hamburger wrappers as well."

"Yes, I did," she said. "I'm doing this exactly why?"

"Because I'm worried about Ms. Guitierrez.

"Hmmm?"

"I had a dream."

"Right, right. You were in a meadow and Susannah turned into plastic or started bleeding or something. Then, the next time you saw her, things were all wrong – whatever. But that's you. My point is, why am *I* doing this?"

"You're my friend."

"I'm your 'get me up at noon so we can go shopping' friend. Hawkins is your 'it's so damn early I can't believe it' friend."

"Hawkins is doing some kind of a church thing."

"At this hour? He's an idiot." Liz closed her eyes. "I'm an idiot, too, I guess. After we see Susannah, you are *so* taking me to breakfast."

Chapter Twenty-Four

Miss Sweet had found them the car a week ago. It was a used two-door sedan, bleached white, and with a deep scratch carved into its rear bumper. It started easily and ran well, it was dependable, and not even the most avid car aficionado would give the vehicle a second glance.

Piece a shit, Mr. Brass thought, as he had when he first saw the car. *I'm ashamed to be seen in it.*

Mrs. Norton took the passenger seat, cranking her window down a quarter turn. She didn't like automobiles, had never driven one as far as he knew. Cars were for going places and she found this one satisfactory for that purpose.

Mr. Brass parked the car two blocks from their destination. He locked the doors manually and the pair of them started down the sidewalk.

He didn't mind walking. Better to walk, anyway, than to be seen in that sorry bucket of bolts.

"It appears we've arrived, Mr. Brass," Mrs. Norton said, touching her finger to the last of the black boxes on a mail stand. At the top was the label, <u>24B</u>. Beneath the number, there was a name: *S Guitierrez.*

Indistinguishable from its neighbors, <u>24B</u> was a two-story row house. Each of the red brick units had its own cement walkway leading into a small courtyard. Every courtyard featured an eight-foot circle of grass and

164

most of them boasted a single tree in the center of the grass enclosure. Hiding behind each courtyard was an entryway with a secluded front door.

They followed the cement pathway to the end unit.

Pressing his eye to the peephole at the front door, Mr. Brass saw only blackness. He jiggled the doorknob but it remained firm and unmoving in his grip.

"What happened to small town values?" he said softly. "Neighbors trusting neighbors?"

He removed a folded leather wallet from his jacket's inner pocket. The wallet unfolded to display a series of lock picks, each nestled in its own sleeve. For the door handle, he selected the next to the smallest pick. For the pair of upper deadlocks, he'd need something bigger.

"Careful," Mrs. Norton said. "We don't want any scratches, even on the strike plate. No damage to the jamb."

She said it as if he was still green. As if he was as raw as Mr. Locke. It bothered him, like the car bothered him, but he knew better than to let his feelings show.

He focused on his task. "Do you remember when we had the locksmith shop? Was there ever a better business for us?" He twisted the bent wire up, up again, and then down. The spring-driven latch released and the handle clicked open.

"It improved your skills."

Thirty seconds later, the door was unlocked. Inside, a semi-circle of polished tile marked the home's entrance. White carpeting flowed into a modest living room on their right and onto the steps of the stairway on their left. From one of the unseen rooms in front of them, a pot gurgled. The smell of fresh coffee was in the air.

On the second floor, a sliver of light shone from beneath a closed door. Inside the room was the muffled sound of running water.

The meat is awake.

Mr. Brass was so hungry he almost didn't care. From experience, he knew he could be up the stairs in seconds. Even if the bathroom door was locked, it wouldn't slow him. Made from plywood or press board, it would shatter beneath the strength of his need.

In less than a minute, he could have his hands on his victim's throat. There was a time, long since passed, when he'd have acted on his desire. Now, he didn't move. Knowing the blood lust was on his face, he waited for Mrs. Norton to speak.

"Quietly," she said.

Disappointment washed over him. Softly, he went up the stairs. At the mouth of the hallway, he paused to listen to the noises around him.

To his left, nothing. To his right, faucets squeaked as the roar of running water diminished and disappeared. He crept to the bathroom door, hearing the sound of flesh rubbing over porcelain. It was followed by a splash and then the sound of water lapping inside the tub.

She was in there, exposed and helpless. He wondered if her eyes were closed. Had she left her bathrobe in a pile on the floor, never to be needed again? Was she in a bubble bath, soap suds floating above the skin of her naked body?

The contemplation of her demise was so delicious he wished he could linger in the hallway, savoring it. But his hunger drove him forward.

The knob turned easily in his grip. Her arms supported on the edges of the bathtub, Susannah Guitierrez gave a startled cry when he entered the room.

I wish I could let you scream, meat, we'd both enjoy it so. But Mr. Brass knew better. Covering Susannah's mouth, he shoved her under the water.

Her eyes had been open when he entered the room. A pink bathrobe hung on the hook inside the door. The water was clear and steaming; there were no soap suds.

Life's mysteries, so easily answered.

Water splashed around him as she squirmed beneath his hold. Susannah's hand shot forward, finding purchase on the side of the bathtub. Her other hand followed, her fingernails scratching uselessly over the arm of her assailant. A nail broke as it struck his vacant forearm, snapping as if it had struck stone.

He sensed another presence in the room. Her eyes bright with interest, Mrs. Norton watched their victim fight for survival.

Susannah's fingers curled over the rim of the bathtub. Bracing her legs in the tub, she propelled herself from the water. Rage in her eyes, she glared at him. Wet and slippery, she twisted from his grasp. Mr. Brass heard a sharp whistle of sound as she sucked in air.

Fiercely, she bit down on his smallest finger. Shock filled her face as her teeth cracked against the unyielding digit. A piece of tooth shattered, falling from her mouth.

"Good effort," Mr. Brass said. Grabbing her hair, he used his other arm to press against the soft folds of her stomach. He forced her body down to the bottom of the bathtub.

167

"Gently," Mrs. Norton said. "There's to be no bruising, no broken skin."

Easy for her to say. This one's a fighter.

She proved it when, flailing, she again found a hold on the slick edges of the tub. He let her face rise from the water. Spreading his fingers, he gave her a single gasp of air before he pushed her down. Her head hit the tub with a dull *thunnnng.*

Five years for one, he thought.

Weaker now, Susannah struggled upward. He let her lift from the bottom of the tub but not quite high enough to break the water. He could feel the bones of her skull as he brought her head down.

Thunnnng.

You've had so many years, he told her silently. *Years of taste and smell and touch. I want my time.*

Give it to me.

Bucking, fighting, she brought her torso out of the water but he kept his palm over her airway. This time, there would be no respite. Enjoying his power, he forced her head down.

Thunnnng.

Her arms trembled as Susannah tried to surface once more. Her hands slipped from their perch, falling into the water. Under his hold, she softened, grew limp.

No paradise for you, meat. Not when you die like this.

No chance for redemption. No hope for salvation. Nothing left for you at all.

Nothing but the Void.

She sank to the bottom of the tub, her eyes open but blind. The lost fragment of tooth lay beside her, trapped between flesh and porcelain. He retrieved it, tucking it inside his shirt's top pocket. A trail of water dribbled after it.

It was nearly time to feed.

Mrs. Norton crept closer. Jealously, he hunched over the body in the tub.

She's hungry, too, he thought with sharp awareness. *What will I do if she chooses to take the meal?*

He knew he dared do nothing. If she wanted to feed, she would.

He darted a sideways glance at her. Delicately taking the broken piece of Susannah's fingernail from the bathroom's linoleum flooring, she put it in her mouth. Swallowing it, Mrs. Norton left the bathroom.

Bending over the tub, Mr. Brass unhinged his jaw. He stretched his mouth wide, and then wider. Inside his throat, he could feel the vortex, whirling.

The greedy beast senses she's close. It's as ready as I am.

The woman's essence rose from her body, no more solid than the morning's mist. As it lifted toward salvation, toward some unseen circle of Heaven's light, he inhaled.

Her presence came into him, *filled* him. He absorbed the five years that should have been: the joy, the happiness, the good health.

He devoured it all.

Color washed into him. Increased sensation arrived and, with it, the sweet arrival of life itself. He could feel his heart pump. He could taste the air he breathed. The clothing covering him suddenly felt wet and cold. His shoes felt too tight around his feet.

He lifted up, filled. For a few short months, his body would be rich with the needs, possibilities and vulnerabilities of the flesh. He rubbed his hands together, one over the other, feeling the friction of his skin. He pressed his fingertips to his face, feeling his nose, his eyelids, his ears. Pursing his lips, he blew across his wrist. Wonderfully, the air coming from his mouth felt warm.

The meat was hollowed, the interior of the bath tub clearly visible through her frame. Inside the shell of her stomach, he saw what was left of her essence. The size and shape of a flower's petal, it shriveled inside of her, curling into itself as it turned from gold to brown.

Then it winked away, leaving nothing behind.

"Sorry," Mr. Brass said, meaning, *I'm sorry I can't do this to you again.*

Not for the first time, he wished his victims could return to life. If the Dark Ones granted him one wish, this is what he would want: the opportunity to kill a mortal, someone such as Susannah Guitierrez, over and over again, year after year, for all of eternity.

Drown her, stab her, shoot her, strangle her. Endless feeding with the same victim, a new manner of murder every time. It was his only fantasy.

From downstairs, there was the sound of the front door opening.

"Ms. Guitierrez?" a female voice called. "Susannah? Are you home?"

"I smell coffee," a second voice said. Female, again. "Let's check the kitchen."

He was searching for a weapon when Mrs. Norton's hand dropped upon his shoulder. Following her, he

170

slipped down the stairway as a light came on in the back of the house. When the two of them went through the open front door, he could hear the intruders talking to one another in the kitchen. Alarm was growing in their voices but it hadn't yet taken hold.

Soon there will be screams.

Following the outcry, there would be sirens, then ambulances, and police cars. People would be panicked, running everywhere.

It would be a wonderful sight.

Mrs. Norton proceeded down the cement walkway. She fussed at her clothing, smoothing the sleeves of her jacket. When she was done, she eyed him critically. "You're wet."

"I can feel it," he said, with pride.

A cry of alarm came from Susannah's house. The sound throbbed with pain. Then – sharp and cutting, piercing the air – a woman screamed.

"I'm going to the main boulevard," Mrs. Norton said. "I'll find a ride. When you're presentable, you'll collect the auto and return to the café."

"Let me get the car now."

"The police are coming. What will you say if a patrol car pulls us over? How are you going to explain your wet clothes?"

"I don't know." Well, what did she expect him to say? He had muscle, he had strength. He wasn't the smart one. "I'll wait, then. Find a place to hide."

"Not here."

Mr. Brass said, "There's one of those storage unit places behind the baseball field. Eastside Storage, maybe

171

a mile from here. Lots of trees, plenty of cover. It would be easy to spend an hour there."

"Very well." Her soft-soled, tan shoes made little noise as she followed the sidewalk.

He touched at his shirt. The fabric was rough and garish. The buttons felt too big between his fingers. His pants weren't any better. They were coarse and cheaply stitched; he should have bought better.

An hour ago, his clothing hadn't mattered. Now that he was alive again, he cared.

He'd find better soon enough. The shirt and pants would be dry by the time he reached the storage yard. If he saw a store in the area, maybe he could go shopping. If not, he'd return and collect the *piece a shit* car.

But was this any way to start this grand, new year, wasting so many minutes on such an unnecessary task?

Still, what choice did he have? He didn't dare return to the café because Mrs. Norton would be waiting there.

Which means, he reflected, *she won't know if I go to the storage unit or not. She doesn't check me for lies, not anymore. She only checks Mr. Locke.*

Did he dare be so bold?

When he heard the first, faint wailing of sirens, he felt happy.

Chapter Twenty-Five

For once, even Liz didn't want to talk. Ear buds fed her music while she sat on the molded plastic chair. She'd redone her make-up twice now, hiding the tracks of her tears. Her eyes remained red.

Kristin sat in the connecting chair beside her. In the Sheriff Station's bathroom mirror, she'd seen the strain on her own face. She didn't worry whether she'd start crying again. She felt as if she'd already used every tear in her body.

Every now and then, Deputy Kane would glance up from her desk and look at them. She'd already taken their reports and shared the results with the Sheriff. She'd have been glad to send them on their way if only Kristin hadn't asked to stay longer.

"Another bathroom slip and fall," one of the paramedics said, wheeling Susannah's body from her house. Kristin wasn't going to let it go so easily. She requested to speak with Sheriff Archer.

"It should only be a few more minutes, girls," Deputy Kane said apologetically. Which was apparently true, or at least it was something the Deputy believed to be true. Talking on the telephone and greeting visitors at the desk, she hadn't lied once since they'd been escorted to the plastic chairs.

Once you see Sheriff Archer, what are you going to say? Kristin asked herself. *Got a plan, some plan, any plan at all?*

Nope. I got nothin'.

If she wanted to be taken seriously, she'd have to watch what she said. Instinctively, Liz understood this, too. Talking to the Deputy, she hadn't mentioned a word of Kristin's dream.

It would remain between the two of them. She wouldn't tell the Sheriff any of it: How things went white when she saw Susannah, how a rasping noise followed her loss of sight, how she smelled the stench of new plastic. All of it, for now and forever, a secret.

Otherwise, no one would believe her.

Sheriff Archer would listen to her because she insisted on being heard, but he knew her history. He'd remember when he was only a Deputy Sheriff and was called by the school to escort her to the Center for the Fractally Whacked.

Kristin leaned over to Liz. Her friend removed one of the plugs from her ear.

"Do you think Deputy Kane told the Sheriff?"

Liz seemed lost at first. Then she said, "You mean, the whole fainting thing?"

"I didn't faint. I *nearly* fainted."

"Close enough." Liz replaced the ear bud. "When we saw Susannah going into the body bag, I wanted to pass out. I was just glad you did it first." Tucking her legs under the chair, she stared off into the distance.

"I didn't pass out," Kristin protested.

174

Tragic as it was, it wasn't Susannah's death that left her feeling weak-kneed. Not directly. It was the body bag itself which made her suddenly feel sick.

To begin with, she'd always thought those types of bags were black, appropriately colored for a mortuary. Now she knew they came in white. She never imagined the bag's zippers were so large and heavy or that their slider rasped so loudly when its teeth bit together. She never realized how strongly a new body bag reeked of a chemical plastic smell.

Too late wise, as her mother would have said. She'd been given the clues, for what little good they did her. She couldn't help but feel she should have done something. Somehow, she should have saved Susannah.

Now my mother's best friend is gone. Dead... and maybe worse than dead.

Transformed.

The body in the tub didn't belong to Susannah any longer. The thing in the water was a hollow shell. Lacking all but the outlines of blood and muscle, organs and flesh, it was as empty as the ghost people who had come to town.

Susannah had been drained and Kristin knew who'd done it.

Mr. Brass.

When the ambulances parked in front of Susannah's house, he was there. Dressed in store label jeans and a five-dollar Hawaiian shirt, he lingered beside the rear doors of the ambulance. He watched with avid interest as the paramedics brought the stretcher out of the row house's front door. Entranced by the body in front of him, he'd never noticed Kristin.

She'd seen him, though. No longer a blank canvas, he now had too-pink skin and dark hair. He showed yellow teeth when he smiled, as he did when the stretcher carrying the body bag bumped over the curb and rolled past him. There were brown freckles on his oversized hands and a white scar running along the side of his neck. His arms were cordoned with heavy veins that existed to feed his thickly-muscled arms.

He wasn't a glass man anymore. Seeing him on the street was like watching some bizarre black-and-white photo newly colorized by the death of a good woman.

How could such a thing happen? She didn't know. But she believed in what she saw and she thought her conclusion was reasonable – if only it hadn't been so impossible.

Too impossible to share with Sheriff Archer or anyone else. Less so, of course, because of her reputation as Winterhaven's very own Mad Hatter.

Deputy Kane lowered the telephone receiver from her ear. "Your grandmother is here, Liz. She's in Visitor Parking."

"I have *got* to get my car back." Tugging out the ear buds, Liz told Kristin, "It is seriously weird to be your friend."

"I'm sorry."

"Me, too. Call. Later."

"Promise."

Liz left through the side exit. A few minutes later, the Deputy gestured toward the Sheriff's office.

Kristin opened the frosted glass door. Squeezed into a shiny black chair, Sheriff Archer sat behind his large wooden desk. "Take a seat, Kristin. Always good to see you."

"Good to see you, too, Sheriff," she said.

"Not like this, though."

"No, never like this."

"Bonnie Kane says you think Susannah's death wasn't an accident." He rested his hand on top of the stack of papers on his desk. "The EMS guys disagree."

"The EMS guys are wrong."

"I was out there maybe an hour ago," he told her. "There wasn't any sign of forced entry."

"The door was unlocked. When Liz and I got to Susannah's house, we walked right in."

"Honey, it's a shock. I know," Archer said. "Doesn't make it murder."

Not knowing what to say, Kristin viewed him stolidly.

He told her, "The way I make it, Susannah got up to start her day. Turned on the coffee, ran the tub. She's ready to get into the water, feels a little dizzy, maybe she passes out. Probably the heart, possibly a CVA. She goes down, sends water everywhere, bangs her head. Drowns. A sadness, without a doubt. I'll cry at her funeral, you know I will. But it was an accident."

"Sheriff...."

He flipped to the second page of the EMS report. "'Minor trauma, consistent with stroke or seizure'. A little bruising around the face. Broke a tooth, probably on the edge of the bathtub." He folded the page back. "You get Susannah's age, things happen. Not always good things."

"Do you remember three years ago?"

"I'm not saying the case ends here," he continued. "I've already contacted the County Coroner. It's protocol. I'll bet you dollars to donuts what he'll find. A lot of water in the lungs, a residue of soap, probably the remainder of one of those Weight Watchers meals Susannah was always eating."

"Three years ago," Kristin said. "The Two Rivers' Convenience Store. Somebody broke in over the weekend. Riffled the cash register, took over four hundred dollars worth of wine and beer."

"I remember."

"Dusty Harrison was blamed for it. He'd lost his job, needed the money. He didn't have an alibi. There were two eyewitnesses placing him at the scene."

"The Galloway sisters," Archer said. "Somehow, you knew Dusty was innocent. Those Galloway girls did it."

"I knew they weren't telling the truth. You listened to me then."

He sighed. "Bonnie says you have a suspect for me. You think, maybe, one of the owners of the new café had something to do with Susannah's death."

"I saw the café's cook outside of the house."

"Before or after the ambulance came?"

"After," she admitted.

"Could just be somebody on ghoul patrol. All it takes is the cry of a siren to bring 'em out. Happens all the time. It's a little disturbed, not criminal."

"He wasn't acting right," Kristin said. The Sheriff raised a questioning eyebrow in her direction. "He seemed pleased with himself. Happy, in a strange way."

"Clothing all wet, buttons missing from his shirt? Any signs he'd been in a struggle?"

"I only saw him for a few seconds."

"So that would be a 'no'." Reaching into his desk drawer, Archer retrieved a notepad. He scribbled something on it. "You know this guy's name?"

"Brass."

"First name?"

"Mister."

"Jesus and Mary, can't you give me a little more than that?" He clipped his pen onto his shirt pocket. "Tell you what. Things slow up here, maybe I'll nose around a little."

He rocked back in his chair, his image growing fuzzy. It shook, faded, then he disappeared into the white wall behind him.

"I'll get his first name, run a background check." Archer's voice spoke from somewhere in front of her. "Nothing official –"

He continued speaking but the words were buried beneath the sound of metal grinding over metal. The stench of plastic filled the office.

"Kristin?"

He popped into view, regarding her curiously. The walls behind him returned, wanted posters pinned to their surface. The rasping noise was gone. "You okay? You're as pale as a ghost."

The smell of plastic lingered in the air.

"Kristin?"

She said, "I need to get home. Mom's probably worried."

"Not a bad idea."

"I was being stupid," she said, rising to her feet. *Not a lie, not today.* After all that had gone on, she didn't think she could stand losing her mouth. "Thinking it over, I mean. The paramedics were there. They wrote their report. If they say it was an accident –" *Careful with your words now* "– then they ought to know."

"You said they made a mistake."

"I'd never seen a dead body before," she said. "I freaked. I'd hate for you to go out to the café. You've got other things to do."

"What about this..." He paused to study the notepad. "Mister Brass?"

"The sirens woke up everybody. Half of the neighborhood came out to watch. If you arrested all of the people who were there, you wouldn't have any room left in the jailhouse."

"Like I said."

"I want you to forget it, okay?"

Archer put a hand to his chin. He rubbed a thoughtful finger over his lower lip.

"Promise," Kristin said.

The Sheriff's face relaxed. Tearing away the top sheet of his notepad, he curled it into a ball. "It's not like I don't have any real crimes to worry about."

He threw the paper ball into the wastebasket at her feet. "Nothing but net!" he cried triumphantly as she closed the door behind her.

* * *

His shift almost over, Sheriff Archer studied the EMS report again. When he was done, he stabbed at the intercom call switch. "Bonnie."

"Sir?"

"You hear back from Carlisle?"

"He's done with the Guitierrez place. Everything's been labeled and bagged. Digital pics are on the computer if you're interested."

"What about his report?"

"It's in there, too."

"Anything I should know about?"

Through the intercom's tiny speaker, Archer heard a rustle of pages. "Nope. Looks like what it was."

"An accident."

"Without a doubt," the Deputy agreed.

He released the intercom button. He pushed back in his seat, feeling its mesh webbing rub roughly across the back of his shirt. "Goddamn chair."

He shouldn't have let Bonnie replace the old chair. Its cloth face was worn, it had lost a little stuffing, but at least it felt like it was made for a man's body.

Its replacement was an unholy creation of mesh, fabric, chrome spindles and plastic. It didn't feel like a chair at all. This five-wheeled waste of money was some kind of NASA-inspired torture device.

"Ergonomic, my ass." Leaning across his desk, he pushed at the intercom button. "Hey, Kane."

"Yes, sir?"

"Did Carlisle ever find that missing piece of tooth?"

Chapter Twenty-Six

Martin Piotrowski slipped the key into his pants pocket before crossing the sidewalk to unlock the mailbox. At the bottom of the container, under a utility bill, several advertisements, and two donation requests was a small envelope.

Feeling his heart quicken, he picked the mail up and carried it inside. Throwing most of the collection into the trash, he placed the envelope on the polished surface of his dining table. Hesitant to read it, he left it there while he showered and shaved.

A towel over his shoulders, Martin walked barefoot into the dining room. Dressed in boxer shorts and a loose t-shirt, he checked for the envelope, suddenly and absurdly frightened it might be gone.

There it is, he thought. *Of course, it is. What did you think? You'd imagined it?*

He examined the white rectangle more closely. His name and home address were written in green letters. It was Chandra's handwriting, as flowing and delicate as ever. She'd used a colored pen, as she often did when writing personal correspondence.

A Lincoln Memorial stamp was affixed to the envelope's upper right-hand corner. Overlying the stamp was its postmark: *Phoenix, Arizona*, dated six days ago. No return address was listed.

His cursory investigation finished, he returned the envelope to the dining room table. It was a little bit of Chandra, ready to be heard, and he'd let her speak. For now, it was her turn to wait.

Filling a cereal bowl with bran flakes and skim milk, he brought it to the table. Eating his breakfast, he wondered what she might have written.

Did she miss him? Did she want to return to Winterhaven? Return to their home, share his bed, build new memories?

He chewed on a mouthful of bran. This wasn't all about Chandra, anymore. Now, what he wanted mattered, too. Did he want her back? She'd left so quickly, barely saying anything.

"I have to find myself." All she had to do was look in a mirror. "I have to find myself." It made no sense. It certainly wasn't reason enough to leave a man, a husband, after forty-one years.

Did he still love her?

I do, he decided, *but there will have to be changes.*

They'd go to counseling, that was a given. There was an experienced marital counselor in Lincoln City, he'd heard some terrific things about her practice. The service was pricey but professionals didn't come cheap. The rent from the café would help with the expense.

They'd both made mistakes. Things might never be as they once were but that didn't mean they couldn't have good times again.

Since she'd finally "found herself" and all.

He pushed the empty cereal bowl aside. Using the edge of his spoon handle, he slit the envelope open. There

183

were three small pages folded inside and he shook them out.

The letter was dated from almost two weeks earlier and Chandra's handwriting filled each page. As with the envelope, there was no return address listed.

"My dearest Martin," he read and his heart fell. He was never her "dearest Martin" unless she needed to share some bad news.

He read through the letter carefully. Chandra wasn't returning home. She loved him and would always love him but not in the old way. They'd had some wonderful years together and she admitted things might have been different if they'd had children – but that was a joy denied them. It had always been just the two of them.

Not even that, now, he thought. *She's building a new life. There isn't anyone else but she doesn't want me, either.*

It's over. We're over.

Everything is over.

He carefully folded the pages closed before tucking them into their sleeve. Not certain where he should store her letter, he left it on the table. He carried his dirty bowl and spoon over to the sink. Rinsing them, he placed them in the dishwasher.

Martin went into the living room and settled into his recliner. Picking up the remote control, he turned on the television. On screen instantly, a pair of talking heads chattered to one another about the previous night's sports scores.

He heard the two men speaking but, for the life of him, he couldn't make any sense of the words they were saying. Burying his face in his hands, he started to cry.

184

* * *

Mr. Brass slammed the hammer down. It struck the nail's head, driving it through the drywall and into the stud behind it. Pinching the nail between his fingers, he checked to see if its bite felt solid. Locked in the wood, it refused to move.

Raising a mirror to the wall, he centered the teeth of its mounting bracket over the nail. Once it was flush with the wall, he released it and admired his handiwork. The mirror stayed in place, holding at face-level and perfectly square.

"Not bad," he told himself.

Mr. Brass grinned at his reflection. He could see every wrinkle, every scar. No matter how he turned his head, he could see his flesh in every detail.

The sight of his own face was a rush.

Carrying a large stainless-steel colander, Mr. Locke entered behind him. "What are you doing?"

"It's a mirror." Mr. Brass tugged at an ear, watching it stretch at the side of his head.

"What a waste." Mr. Locke thumped the colander onto a prep table.

"It would be for you," he agreed. "What would you use it for? To look at the walls behind you? To stare through your face at the walk-in refrigerator?"

He laughed. Opening his shirt, he ran a hand over the black hair on his chest. "The first few weeks always feel so good. Sometimes you forget how good it can feel."

"Seems like you forget about the smell, too. I can smell the flesh on you. The stench of humanity. You stink like they do."

"Hungry?" Mr. Brass remained at the mirror. It was a pleasure to watch his red lips move, to see the yellow of his teeth when they parted. "I'll bet you are. I'll bet you're starving. It's been such a long time."

Mr. Locke remained at the table, unmoving. He stared down at the colander, hatred carved into his face.

"It's worse when you're new. The need is sharper. The desire to feed claws at you, doesn't it?"

Nothing from the pupae. He refused to meet his eyes.

"You need to look at me, Mr. Locke," he said. "Look at my mouth. I want you to see me talk. I want you to know I'm telling the truth."

Mr. Locke lifted his head.

Mr. Brass said, "Mrs. Norton told me, we're not in a hurry here. We'll take our time. We want to enjoy our stay in Winterhaven."

"That all? You done?"

"Not quite," Mr. Brass told him. "You know what else she said?" He leaned forward. "You. Feed. Last."

Mr. Locke slammed his fist, striking the colander. It flew from the table, tumbling across the room. By the time it struck the floor, Mr. Locke was rushing out of the building.

Mr. Brass turned to the mirror. He blew against the glass, watching it fog in front of him.

It's a wonderful life.

* * *

186

Plumping the pillow under her head, Kristin rolled over on her bed.

How many worst days of your life is one person supposed to have, anyway? she wondered. *Shouldn't there be a limit on this kind of thing?*

The first time she could remember having the worst day of her life was in the fourth grade. It was a Wednesday afternoon and the Trio of Evil chased her home, throwing rocks at her the whole way. While her neighbors delighted in the notoriety of Winterhaven's very own town triplets, Kristin lacked their sense of civic pride. She'd never been happier than when the moving trucks arrived to carry Cindy, Carla and Cassandra Dougherty away from her elementary school and off to Wareham, Massachusetts.

Another "worst day" was the Monday she was admitted to Kendall Sanitarium. That particular day, immediately and impossibly, grew even more terrible, turning into the worst year of her life.

But I'm tired of thinking about you, Dr. Ron. Not tonight.

She'd experienced the worst evening of her life during the Junior Prom. Hawkins was her date and, modestly, she thought she looked fairly spectacular. For her, anyway, her particular kind of spectacular. But it turned out, she'd read his signals as badly as possible. Before the end of the evening, he'd been forced to give her the Best Friends Forever speech.

He said he liked her more than any other girl he'd ever met but not in THAT way. He'd only taken her to the prom because she'd asked – and because Lisa McCarthy had broken up with him three weeks earlier. Their mutual embarrassment had been intense.

Fortunately, by the end of the evening, BFF had prevailed. When the night was over, they'd even gone bowling together. It was almost fun in a *Let's-burn-the-prom-pictures* kind of way.

The Trio was bad, Doctor Ron was terrible, and the prom had left an emotional scar. But none of them qualified as the very worst day of her life. The absolute pinnacle of awful had arrived yesterday.

Finding Susannah's body, almost invisible in the tub, was a horrible thing. Talking to Sheriff Archer and experiencing another vision was troubling, too. Coming home to find her mother sobbing had only deepened the tragedy.

As soon as she entered the house, her mother had clutched at her, devastated by the loss of her friend and frightened about the possible damage to Kristin's psyche. The two of them sat together, weeping for hours. It was definitely a ten on the one to ten scale, her most terrible, horrible, no good, very bad day.

She rolled onto her side to look at the bedside alarm clock. *Almost noon.* She still felt exhausted.

She heard a noise from downstairs. It sounded like her mother and Martin Piotrowski.

Dressing quickly, she splashed water over her face before scraping a brush through her hair. In the living room, her mother was standing by the sofa, talking to a man in a black suit.

"Mister Piotrowski?"

Seeing her, he smiled wanly. Kristin felt alarmed. In the few days since they'd last met, he seemed to have aged ten years.

"I've been telling him about Susannah," Becky said.

Martin raised his arms and Kristin went to him. He squeezed her tightly. Within his embrace, she heard him choke back a sob.

"And we have another visitor." Becky stepped aside, allowing Kristin to see the glass frame of a middle-aged woman. "This is Mrs...." Her words trailed off.

"Norton," Mrs. Norton said. "Kristin and I have met before. She came to the café."

"Mrs. Norton. How could I forget? Mrs. Norton." To her daughter, Becky said, "She's been to my gallery."

"Several times now."

"She likes my new work. Not my landscapes, my serious work. She wants me to paint her portrait."

Becky angled her body so only Kristin could see what was in her hands. Excitedly, she revealed a piece of paper. It was a check with a large number written in the dollar column. Mrs. Norton's signature was at the bottom of the check.

"You should know, I'm fairly particular in my tastes," Mrs. Norton warned. "It may take weeks and weeks for us to get things the way I like them."

"That's fine with me," Becky said, creasing the check in half and half again. "We can take as long as you like." Sliding the square of paper into the front pocket of her jeans, she turned to her client. "Is there a Mr. Norton?"

"Not anymore." Mrs. Norton met Kristin's eyes. "I ate him."

Her crystalline face never wavered. Stumbling back, Kristin collapsed onto the sofa. "She – she's not lying."

Becky and Martin laughed politely.

"Anyone for fresh pumpkin bread?" Becky asked, heading for the kitchen.

189

"Love some," Martin said.

Mrs. Norton waited until they'd left. To Kristin, she said, "Your home suffers from a lack of style, doesn't it? It really could use a decorator's hand."

Kristin remained on the sofa. "I like it."

"It's rude to tell others when a person is lying," Mrs. Norton said. "You should have learned this by now."

"I guess I'm a little slow."

"I know, dear. I expect everyone does." She checked to see if Becky or Martin were returning. "I think your mother is a talented artist."

Schhhct! Her mouth blurred as plates of glass dropped in front of it.

"Why must you be such a bother?" Mrs. Norton asked, the words muffled behind their barrier before – *Schhhct!* – her mouth reappeared. "You come to my restaurant and worry my staff. You snoop about. You think you're clever when, really, you're nothing but an aggravation. Too foolish to let well enough alone."

Kristin stayed very still upon the sofa. Her heart thumped inside her chest, beating fast.

"I came here to keep an eye on you. I thought we might come to... an accommodation. A fool's errand, I'm afraid. You censor yourself so poorly. Just now, you didn't have the slightest hesitation in telling the others what you'd seen. That won't do. That won't do at all."

Mrs. Norton let a disappointed frown tug at her mouth. "In centuries past, the town elders would have burned your kind as a witch. I'd have helped them light the pyre."

"I know what you are." The words escaped from Kristin in a whisper.

190

"No, you don't, girl. You only think you do." She stretched a clear hand out to her. "Let's join the others in the kitchen. Don't you want some pumpkin bread?"

Chapter Twenty-Seven

Although he hadn't run patrol in years, Sheriff Archer believed he still knew every alley and side street in Winterhaven. Even if he was flattering himself, he remembered this particular dirt road well. He'd made his first collar here. He could still visualize Aaron Peters, his rear end sticking half out the window of Tyler Feed and Grain while a ten-dollar burglar alarm whistled over his head.

Poor Aaron Peters, always one DUI away from a steady job. Now he was every bit as dead and gone as Tyler Feed and Grain itself.

Old Tom Tyler had gotten sick and sold out, letting a bait-and-tackle shop take over the property; in due time, the bait-and-tackle shop was replaced by Martin Piotrowski's restaurant. Only the grain store had enjoyed any kind of success. Even in its heyday, Tom Tyler hadn't cared enough to build any kind of barrier to secure his property.

The newest owners, though, they've built one heck of a fence, Archer thought. *Then, when they finished with it, they dug deep into their wallets to buy a top-of-the-line tubular key lock to pin the gates closed. Seems like a lot of protection for such a modest enterprise.*

Not that the lock or the fence was doing the café's owners any good at this particular moment. On this day, early in the morning, the fence's double gates were wide open.

Ain't it the way? No matter what you want to protect, no matter what you hope to hide, you can't do much about trash day. Doors have to be opened if you want the sanitation crew to bring in their big brown trucks and empty the dumpsters.

Parking the patrol car in the alley, he got out to check the premises. A double-wide dumpster sat beside the fence on a hard-packed dirt surface. The rest of the area was empty. Empty of life, empty of weeds, empty of a single piece of litter on the ground.

Empty of clues.

He wondered if he was wasting his time. Was there even a crime for him to investigate?

Susannah Guitierrez was still on ice, waiting for the Country Coroner to appear. The only thing unusual about her death was her missing tooth. It wasn't much to go on. She could have broken it a half-dozen different ways before losing it down the disposal or flushing it down the toilet. Even if she'd lost it as a result of her headlong plunge toward the bathtub, its disappearance remained a weak mystery.

She probably swallowed it, he thought. *Unless the coroner orders an autopsy, nobody's gonna see that piece of enamel again.*

Unwilling to abandon his quest so quickly, he approached the dumpster. His nose wrinkled as the smell of decayed food greeted him. Holding his breath, he inspected the empty produce boxes and browned lettuce leaves filling the container.

193

"What'd you think you'd find in there, anyway?" he asked himself, letting the lid drop. "Susannah's gold filling?"

A tall man appeared at the rear service door, watching him. Framed in the doorway, he said, "This is private property."

"I'm Sheriff Archer."

"Is that supposed to impress me?" Hefting a large garbage bag, the man drew closer. "What's it take to be elected sheriff in this county, anyway? How many asses you gotta kiss?"

Oh, I definitely don't like this one. "What's your name, friend?"

The tall man threw open the dumpster's lid. "None of your business, *friend*. Not that your kind knows when to mind its own business."

"My kind?" The Sheriff felt his shoulders stiffen. "What 'kind' is that? The black kind?"

"The kind who go digging through other people's rot. Rutting through their trash."

Archer's hand dropped to the butt of the baton at his waist. He looped his fingers through its leather thong. "Maybe we should have a private talk."

"Downtown? Or right here, right now, just you and me?"

"Mr. Locke!" It was a girl's voice, thin but sharp. The speaker, every bit as thin as her voice, hurried out of the restaurant.

Irritably, the man asked, "What do you want, Alice Poe?"

194

"We need you in the kitchen." The girl glanced at the Sheriff, anxiety filling her face. "We need you to be... inside. Not here."

On closer inspection, Archer realized this person, this Alice Poe, was no longer a girl. She was probably in her late twenties, maybe early thirties, and, he thought uncharitably, nobody's idea of a beauty. She was skin and bones, had nothing in the way of breasts, and barely carried enough in her hips to escape being mistaken for a boy.

To Mr. Locke, Alice Poe said, "Please."

"Yeah." Mr. Locke dropped the bag of trash at Archer's feet. "I can always take care of the garbage later."

"Later can be arranged." He relaxed his grip on his baton.

Mr. Locke sauntered into the building, his shoulders wide and his arms swinging. He wasn't just talking. He was ready for a fight.

Doesn't take much to provoke this one, the Sheriff thought. *Might be fun to watch him dance at the end of a Taser's wire.*

Alice Poe remained with the Sheriff. "Is everything okay?"

"Afraid not." She acted pained by this response. "Tell me where I can find Mr. Brass."

"He's not here."

"I didn't ask where he wasn't." Archer reached into his pants pocket. He withdrew a pen and notepad.

"He's in Ashfork," she said. "He had to drive Mrs. Norton to the import shop."

"Mrs. Norton?"

195

"She owns the café."

He scribbled the name down. "Mr. Brass have a first name?"

"Stephen." Alice Poe's face twitched in mild panic. Her fingers played over her lips, almost as if she was touching something.

Be interesting to see how this one does with a drug test. A strange little bird, that's for sure. "When will Stephen Brass return?"

"Return? To the café?"

"No, to my house." On her bewildered expression, he said, "Yes, here. At the restaurant. This is where he lives, right? Where all of you live?"

"He'll be home soon. Tonight, I think."

"Then why don't I come back tonight?" Closing the notepad, he returned it to his pocket. "Would this be okay with you, Alice?"

At his question, her eyes flared with anger. She puffed up her tiny chest, so mad she couldn't – or wouldn't – speak.

Alice Poe and Mr. Locke were quite the curious pair. He wondered if Mr. Brass and Mrs. Norton could possibly prove half as interesting.

He wondered, too, what was really going on at Piotrowski's Café.

Touching the brow of his hat, he nodded at the woman. "See you later, then."

* * *

Sitting on the edge of her bed, Kristin hit redial on her cell phone. From the other end, she heard a ring.

196

Almost immediately, the Reverend Howard Hawkins' voice came on the line: *"We're not home right now. At the tone, leave a message and may God be with you."*

His voice was followed by a sharp, short *beep*.

She ended the transmission. Having left three messages without a response, she didn't see any reason to leave another.

"I'm in serious distress here, Hawk."

The night before, she'd driven past Hawkins' house. The outside porch light was on but the house was dark. She'd even driven to the Galilee Church which, without front lights, appeared gloomier still.

This morning, neither Hawkins was answering the telephone. She couldn't even call Hawk's cell phone. The last she'd seen of it, it was squirting out of his hand and plunging to the bottom of Vulture's Gorge.

Liz, too, was ignoring her. Liz, who counted food, air, make-up and cell phones among the necessities of modern life, suddenly couldn't be bothered to respond to a text message. From all appearances, the ever-available Liz Wheeler had gone incommunicado.

What do I do now?

There were bad, evil creatures in Winterhaven and no one knew it but her. The ghost people had already claimed Susannah Guitierrez's life. Now Mrs. Norton was making arrangements to come into her home, twice a week, for who knew how long.

Maybe if she stayed quiet, they'd go away. If she pretended not to notice them, maybe they'd pretend to ignore her.

Unless it was already too late.

197

Mrs. Norton had made it clear she wasn't happy with Kristin. Nor were any of the others. From her observations, she thought Mr. Locke was the most aggressive and Mr. Brass appeared the strongest. But their middle-aged master scared her the most.

Did she plan to drain her like Mr. Brass drained Susannah? Or did they have a different victim in mind? Like, maybe, her mother?

I've got to do something about them, she thought. *But what? There's nothing I can do by myself.*

I have to get help.

Not Sheriff Archer, no. She couldn't stand the sight of another body bag, thank you. Her mother? No chance. She'd want to believe her but she wouldn't. Couldn't.

No one could, probably.

With her history, anyone in authority would want to surround her with psychologists and counselors. They'd try to fix her by giving her another year's vacation in the rubber room. While she was locked up, Mrs. Norton and her family would be free to feast upon the people she loved.

Liz and Hawkins wouldn't believe her story, either, but at least they'd listen to her. Liz was always reading books about telekinesis and spontaneous combustion and other pseudoscientific nonsense so she might be open to her story.

Or she might punch the speed-dial for the guys in the white coats. With Liz, it was hard to say.

Hawkins was different. Of her two best friends, he was her *best*, best friend. Indoctrinated in the Good Book, he'd grown up believing in supernatural forces and miracles. Why should one more fantastical tale bother him? Were ghostly killers any less believable than a burning bush that talked or someone turning into a pillar of salt?

Okay, maybe so. But he had to believe her, anyway. *Someone* had to believe her. Or she really would go crazy.

There was one more number she could dial. It wouldn't get her any closer to Hawkins but it was a direct link to Liz.

Suck it up, she told herself. *After all, maybe Liz is sick. Maybe she's had her cell phone cut off. Only one way to find out.*

Quit being a coward. Dial the number.

On the other end of the airwaves, the phone rang once before a frail, reedy voice responded. "Hello?"

"Nana Beggio?" she asked. "This is Kristin. Kristin Faraday. I'm trying to find Liz."

Thirty minutes later, she disconnected the call. Liz wasn't answering because she was in summer school. Each calculus class was a four-hour math marathon followed by a short lunch break and another two-hour study session. Dr. Silva prohibited cell phones in his classroom. If he heard the first chirp of a ring tone, the unfortunate student involved could count on his or her latest homework score dropping by ten percentage points.

She'd learned this gush of information within the first five minutes of her call. Nana Beggio used the rest of the time to share the long and involved history of her arthritis pain, her dry skin, and a few of the challenges involved in owning a free-spirited cat and a half-deaf bulldog named Winston. In the end, solely to get off of the telephone, Kristin promised to visit the Beggio house within the next two weeks.

Nana Beggio couldn't have been more pleased. "Why, we can talk for hours."

Bottom-line, Liz isn't available. Hawkins has disappeared. If you're going to do something, you'll have to figure it out on your own.

"Damn it!" Kristin threw her cell phone.

It smacked into the opposite wall, its red cover plate snapping off on impact. It fell onto the carpet, a dent visible in the upper corner of its aluminum body.

The cell phone rang.

She looked at it blankly. *Is this what happens when a cell phone breaks? Is this a last jingle of protest?*

It rang again. Scrambling from her bed, she grabbed it. "Hello?"

"Hey dere, hi dere, ho dere."

"Hawkins!"

"Got my new phone," he said. "It even has quasi-decent reception from Oklahoma City."

"Where are you?"

"At the seminary," Hawkins said. "Shaking hands, filling out forms, signing papers." He sounded proud of himself. "By mid-September, I'll officially be a second-generation Oklahoma Trinity college student."

"When will you be back?"

"Tomorrow morning. Red of eye and full of caffeine, I'm teaching Dad's Bible class at church."

"Bible class?" Kristin said. "It's Saturday."

"Dad always teaches a class on Saturday. About fifty weeks of the year, anyway. Tomorrow, I'm at the podium."

"Can you skip it?"

"My first class? No way." In the background, she heard his father say, "Roaming charges, Gideon, roaming charges! Hang up!"

"I really need to talk."

"Roaming charges, Kristin, roaming charges," Hawkins said. "Gotta go."

"Wait," she told him. "When will you get back to the church?"

"My church? You'd meet me at my church?"

"What time?"

"Ten o'clock, give or take."

"I'll be there."

* * *

Hawkins flipped his cell phone closed. "Well, well," he said. "Hallelujah, indeed."

Chapter Twenty-Eight

Sheriff Archer wondered if he should have changed into street clothes before returning to the café. If this were a social visit, he decided, that's just what he'd have done. For now, though, it was better to stay in his blues. It was a way to remind the jittery Alice Poe that he represented truth, justice, and the American way. At least, to the extent that the good people of Winterhaven still believed in such things.

Somewhere inside the first story of the building, a light glowed. Upstairs, a smear of yellow flame flickered back and forth. He didn't need to see the *Sorry, We're Closed* sign in the window to tell him the restaurant was shut down for the day.

Rubbing his badge with his sleeve, he climbed the porch and knocked at the front door. It was his polite knock, three taps and done.

If his call went without answer, he'd use his Sheriff's knock. Then he'd drum on the door with such power that it shook the wood beneath his fist. It almost always elicited an urgent, usually frightened, response.

The door opened in front of him. The reed-like Alice Poe said, "Evening, Sheriff."

He brought an index finger and thumb to the brow of his hat. "Good evening, Alice" – and saw her face tighten almost instinctively. "May I come in?"

She continued to block the doorway. "Mr. Brass isn't back yet. He probably won't return until morning."

"Him and his boss, right?" Archer shifted, trying to peer past this shadow of a woman. "I haven't been in Piotrowski's since it changed ownership."

"There haven't been many changes. Hardly any."

From the dining area, he saw the pretty boy, Mr. Locke, coming their way. "I'd appreciate a look around if you don't mind."

Mr. Locke filled the space behind Alice Poe. When he rested his hand on her shoulder, she softened, melting with pleasure from the contact.

"Got a warrant?" Mr. Locke asked.

"A warrant? Now, why would I need a warrant?" Archer was surprised to feel the cold base of his metal baton touch his palm. He didn't remember reaching for it.

"Typical."

"This isn't an official visit, is it?" Alice Poe asked. "There's nothing to see. Really, there isn't. Mr. Locke and I are the only ones here."

"Don't forget Miss Sweet." When Locke mentioned her name, some strange mischief filled his head. Archer could practically see the gears grinding. "Although she's easily forgettable, our Miss Sweet."

Alice Poe shook her head, either in response to the statement or to stop Mr. Locke from saying anything more.

"Who's Miss Sweet?"

"The café's fortune-teller," Mr. Locke said.

Sheriff Archer felt a smile grow on his face.

Alice Poe said, "Not for money, Sheriff. She does her readings for free."

"Free isn't a crime, is it?" Mr. Locke asked.

He knows it isn't, Archer thought.

"If you'd like to get your fortune told," Mr. Locke continued, "we'll invite you in."

A twitch of fear crossed Alice Poe's brow. It was probably this display of anxiety that decided his next step.

The Sheriff removed his hat. "Might be fun."

* * *

It was ten o'clock and Liz still hadn't called. Her summer class had ended hours ago and, for whatever reason, she was ignoring her text messages. She was ignoring her voice mail, too.

Could she be busy, studying?

Liz? Not a chance. Sighing, Kristin entered Nana Beggio's phone number.

After a single ring, the old woman picked up. She said, "Sweetie, I'm sure I told you. All of Doctor Silva's more challenged students are having a sleep-over."

"A sleep-over?"

"At the professor's house," Nana Beggio said. "They're playing math games all night long. Calculus flip cards, calculus Pictionary. They must be having so much fun."

"Liz agreed to this? Our Liz?"

"She needs the help. The final exam is tomorrow, you know."

"Ahhhhh." *Now* it made sense. "Goodnight, Nana Beggio." Before Nana Beggio could start another sentence, Kristin disconnected the call.

I'll see her soon enough, she thought with the faintest twinge of guilt. *We'll talk then.*

204

Or, more accurately, she'll talk, I'll listen.

Pushing her ear buds in place, she turned on her music player. What was it Nana Beggio had said? "Calculus Pictionary"?

Was Dr. Silva really going to play a game combining Liz's complete disinterest in math with her serious lack of artistic ability? If so, her friend was in for a surprise.

For the first time that day, Kristin relaxed. No matter how bad things seemed, it could be worse. She could be at a math sleep-over and about to discover the joy of playing Calculus Pictionary.

With music playing in her ears, she fell asleep.

* * *

On the second floor, Sheriff Archer went through the first door to his left. It was a small room and dark inside; darker, anyway, than his aging eyes preferred. With Mr. Locke and Alice Poe following him, he coughed to announce his presence.

An old woman sat on the floor, a small table in front of her. Candlelight flickered from three wavering wicks, throwing unkind shadows on her face.

Christ almighty, Archer thought. *You need a movie witch, I've found your girl. This Miss Sweet could have come straight from Central Casting.*

Mr. Locke spoke from over his shoulder. "The Sheriff has come for a reading."

Miss Sweet asked, "Does Mrs. Norton approve?"

"She hasn't returned. Sheriff says he won't leave without a reading."

The hag nodded, tilting her chinless head toward the table. Whatever her thoughts, she hid them from view.

"Tarot cards, right?" Archer said. "Or a Ouija board, maybe a crystal ball. Parlor games for the gullible."

The insult brought her face up. "I play no games."

"Sugar, it's all you know."

"Sit," she told him.

Aware of Alice Poe and Mr. Locke behind him, he closed the door in their surprised faces.

"I like my room open," Miss Sweet said.

"See, that's where I disagree with you. I prefer a little privacy. Since I'm the client with the badge, we'll do it my way." Sliding his legs under the table, he laid his hat on the floor beside him.

Looking like she'd bitten into a lemon, the fortune-teller reached across the table. "Give me your hand."

He stretched it out. The old woman held his open palm over the center of the table, directly above a long, black rock. Archer was still in her grip when her other hand flashed forward. Something bit into his finger.

"Owww!" He tried to pull away as her hand tightened over his. "Let go of me."

She twisted his wrist and he saw a large drop of blood tremble on the tip of his finger. "I ask only for the smallest sacrifice. Do you give it?"

"My blood? You want my blood?"

She waited, her eyes like onyx pebbles.

"Do it," Archer said. "I'm here. I might as well see your voodoo."

The red droplet fell, spreading over the rock. The rock seemed to glow as she released him.

206

"Before the future, the past," Miss Sweet said. "I see your father was a policeman." She waved a hand over the stone. "Your father's father wore blue as well."

"Not exactly a revelation," he told her. "Cops run in my family. As long as there's been a Winterhaven, there's been an Archer boy with a badge on his chest. Anybody could have told you as much."

Unperturbed, she remained focused on the stone. Through some trick of the candlelight, the rock changed color under her gaze. "Once you loved your work. Now, your heart is heavy."

"You ever hang out with a bunch of cops? Burn-out happens. Occupational hazard in my line of work."

"For others, yes. Never before for you."

He scooted away from the table. "Begging your pardon, Miss Sweet, but this is getting a little New Age-y for me. Only thing missing is the wind chimes."

"You shouldn't go," she said, "until you've seen the life ahead of you."

Despite himself, Archer leaned forward. *What do you think you'll find in there? This isn't a high-def TV. It's a damned lava rock.*

But he looked down at it, regardless.

Miss Sweet said, "I see five years before you."

"Five?"

"Hard years. Bitter years. The corruption is spreading inside of you."

"Sweet Mother Mary, does anybody ever buy this line of happy horseshit?"

"In your heart, you know it's true."

He brought his eyes up, searching her face. It appeared as cold as the stone beneath her fingers.

207

"You've suspected for a while but you were frightened to act," she continued. "Too late now, much too late. You've always been strong but your strength is fading. Soon, you'll suffer."

"I don't know what you're talking about." Taking his hat, Archer returned it to his head.

"I give you the truth."

"Lady, as old as you are, maybe you're still new to the bunco game. Let me tell you something. There's no coin in an ugly story." Candlelight swayed around him. "To get my money, you're supposed to promise me things. Romance or money or maybe the condo in Vero Beach I've always wanted. You're supposed to tell me all the pretty lies I want to hear."

"I said you had five years."

"Five bad years? Like that's some prize?" he asked. "Or maybe you're playing things a different way. Maybe you want to scare me. For the right price, you'll do a little spell, and suddenly I'm healed. The corruption disappears. Is that it?"

Miss Sweet picked up the fallen stick pin. "You know better."

"Bull." Seeing the pin, he looked down at his injured finger. He blinked his eyes rapidly, as if coming out of a daze. "You stuck me. You took a pin and stuck me!"

With a flick of her finger, Miss Sweet sent the pin flying into the corner waste basket. It made a *dink!* sound as it fell atop a dozen of its twins. Leaning forward, she blew out the first of the candle flames.

"I've had enough." Archer's thumb found the puncture site and massaged it loosely. "I've never had much truck with people like you. I don't like how you

208

operate and I don't much like this place." He reached down to dust his pants. "When your boss arrives, tell her I'm contacting the County Attorney. Between us, I'm guessing we can find reason enough to shut you down."

He threw the door open. Mr. Locke was in the hallway, waiting for him.

"Get the hell out of my face," Archer said.

"How many years?"

"What?"

"How many years did she say you had?"

From the room behind him, Miss Sweet said, "Five years."

"Five years," Mr. Locke repeated, honeyed pleasure in his voice.

"There's more," Miss Sweet said.

Mr. Locke came closer, wanting to hear her message. Archer shoved at the man's chest. "Move."

Mr. Locke felt surprisingly heavy but the push pushed him aside. It gave the Sheriff enough space to escape the gypsy's room.

Abandoning Miss Sweet, Mr. Locke shadowed him. Archer was at the top of the stairway when he felt a hand fell on his shoulder. "Hey, cop."

Turning, the Sheriff saw a flash of silver. He brought his arms up as Mr. Locke slammed a chrome-covered pipe against the side of his head.

A thousand colors erupted within his mind's eye. Archer fell backwards, the stairs racing up to meet him. There was another burst of color as his head hit the top stair.

Then everything went black.

* * *

Mr. Locke felt such power as the meat collapsed, its skull striking the edge of the top step. The body gave a spasm when it hit the floor, bouncing and rolling down the stairway. A smear of blood marked the police officer's progress to the bottom of the landing.

The cascade of noise brought Alice Poe from her room. As useless as ever, she stopped when she saw what had happened, her hands fluttering in fear and indecision. He heard Miss Sweet call out but he ignored her.

The greedy cow can fill herself later. This one belongs to me.

He raced down the steps, his shoes streaked in blood. The meat jerked, sending the vortex inside Mr. Locke's throat whirling in hungry anticipation. Ready and eager, he spread his arms to embrace the feeding.

Nothing happened.

Beneath him, the meat's chest rose and fell. Somehow, it had survived the beating. Its head lolled sideways and its right eye blinked open.

He's strong. Good, good.

Mr. Locke raised his arm. He heard the pipe whistle as he swung his fist downward. The metal bit into flesh, cracking the skull and spraying his victim's blood into the air.

Pinpoints of red sprinkled over him as brain and bone slapped wetly at the bottom of his trousers. He didn't care. Outside of his control, he felt his jaw drop and his mouth extend.

Now, it was his time. *Now*, he could feed.

The life force rose to meet him. In shimmering waves, it surrounded him, falling onto him. It filled him.

Was there ever a more glorious feeling than this?

Sensation crowded around him. Suddenly, the smell of spilled blood filled the air, thick and cloying. It teased him and his mouth watered. He felt vibrantly alive.

Lifting the chrome-covered pipe, he admired his reflection. Spots of blood were scattered over the beautiful brown of his face. He watched himself bring his fingertips to his full, pink lips. He watched his fingers drag streaks of blood along his strong jaw line. It felt wet and even this wetness felt wonderful.

He had regained his color. He was strong and beautiful.

There were so many things he wanted to do. Things he'd stopped doing as their pleasures faded. Everything was different now. *He* was different now.

He wanted to taste food, to eat so much he vomited. He longed for a cigarette, wanting to feel his lungs burn. He'd drink liquor until he couldn't stand. Most of all, he hungered for sex: Dirty, hard, raw sex.

There were times when the others talked about the pleasures of the flesh but he never heard them speak of fornication. Well, Alice Poe did, but only in whispers and only when they were alone. Making promises for when she was filled.

As if he'd desire her even then.

"Oh, no." It was her voice whimpering from the stairs above, the faint words filled with fear and regret. Alice Poe gripped the top of the half-wall. Miss Sweet waited beside her.

211

"He was nothing," he said, not liking how they looked at him. "Less than nothing."

Miss Sweet said, "He wasn't meant to be taken."

"Because he's the Sheriff?" he asked, not bothering to hide the disdain in his voice. "*Was* the Sheriff? He has one deputy, a woman. Who cares? The only thing more useless than meat is female meat."

"That's not what I said."

He snorted derisively. "Because it wasn't my turn, then?" He laughed, enjoying the full, rich sound as it erupted from his mouth. "It would have been my turn soon enough."

"He wasn't whole," Miss Sweet said.

Fear stabbed at his sense of elation. "You said he had five years."

"He did. Five full years. Not good years."

"Why didn't you say?" Mr. Locke demanded. "You dumb, worthless –"

Suddenly, his left side tore at him. Gasping, he clutched for the stairway banister to keep himself from falling.

"He carried disease," Miss Sweet said.

Alice Poe's face was drawn. "It comes quickly for our kind."

Trying to straighten, Mr. Locke felt his feet slide out from him. His right hand splashed through fleshy matter before it found the floor.

He raised his head. "What now?"

"Agony. Despair."

"I heard 'five years'!" Mr. Locke shouted up at her.

"There was more to hear than those few words." Miss Sweet shook her head. "When someone returns

212

from the Void, there are things they think they remember. Funny how much the pit steals from you."

"Make an effort, ancient beast. Try to make sense."

"It takes a day to remember how to eat, a week to talk, and a month to walk. You're still learning. You can't do as much as you think."

"I can do more than you know. Something you can't. Something Mrs. Norton can't do, either." His discomfort easing, he managed a sneer. "I can drive a car."

Alice Poe covered her face with her hands. Her eyes blurred through the layers of her fingers as she tried to hide from Miss Sweet's gaze.

Miss Sweet said, "There are so many things you don't understand."

"Like what?"

"Mrs. Norton," Alice Poe said from behind her hands.

"Her? What can she do to me now?" He pushed himself upright, using the wall as support. "She returned me to this body but she can't take me out of it. You're all so scared of her – and for what? There are few things here that can kill us. Mrs. Norton isn't one of them."

"There are worse things than dead," Miss Sweet said.

Mr. Locke felt a tremor run through his legs. *From the pain*, he thought.

"Run," Alice Poe told him.

He saw pity and fear and desire etched across her face. No matter what he did, she'd follow him.

"Come with me." He put his hand out. "We'll see the world. We'll take what we want instead of letting others tell us what we can have."

Not answering, Alice Poe ran down the hallway.

213

"That's it?" he called after her. "I don't even get a good-bye, you empty bitch?"

From the upper floor, her bedroom door slammed shut. Only Miss Sweet stayed in place, looming over him.

"Why are you still here?" he asked.

"Would you like me to tell your fortune?"

"Shut up."

She cocked her head, watching him.

"Without your rock, you're nothing," he said. "Less than nothing. Certainly less –" He straightened the collar on his shirt, "– than me."

Kicking at the meat, Mr. Locke rolled it over. Sweat beaded across his forehead as he bent to take the Sheriff's wallet and gun. Clutching at his stomach, he stumbled from the kitchen.

He would run, just as Alice Poe had suggested. But there was one thing he needed to do first.

Chapter Twenty-Nine

Hawkins' eyes were burning and it felt like there was grit clawing at each of his eyelids. The only thing keeping him awake was his unhappy bladder. It demanded he leave the car, find the nearest tree, and pee for the next hour or so.

Inconvenient or not, he'd have to answer Nature's call soon. Given a choice, he'd prefer to do it in a well-lit gas station bathroom instead of hiding behind some leafless dogwood tree.

Of course, if things had worked out as planned, he wouldn't have been on the road at all. Registration at the seminary would have been completed by noon if he hadn't had to fill out every financial application in the world.

"No money, no entry," the front clerk told him. The clerk's philosophy didn't seem Christian at all.

By the time he was ready to leave the campus, the evening street lights were coming on. Hawkins suggested they spend the night in Oklahoma City. Predictably, his father refused just as their car passed a Super 8 Motel.

After all, the Pastor Hawkins said, if they drove all night, they could still make the Saturday Bible class in Winterhaven. A Bible class attended by a half-dozen retirees and his father's new girlfriend. Soon-to-be girlfriend, anyway. Not that this had anything to do with it.

"They're counting on us," his father told him, the Super 8's illuminated sign disappearing from their rearview mirror. "It's the right thing to do, Gideon. We have to do the riiiiiiiiiight thing."

Okay, he hadn't said it exactly like that. But he'd said it.

It wasn't as if the old women waiting for them didn't know the story of Jonah and the whale. ("The big fish," said the Reverend, knowing full well Hawkins could quote the scriptures, too, chapter and verse. "There's no mammal in the story. It's Noah and the big fish.") He was pretty sure the matriarchs of the class, Jolene and Jewell, were qualified to step up to the chalkboard if Hawkins and Son failed to make a timely appearance.

The real reason they were on the road? His father wanted the pleasure of seeing his son take his first steps toward becoming a preacher. It was touching, in an aggravating, sleep-deprived kind of way.

"Dad?"

His father's eyelids remained shut. His breathing was deep and relaxed. Somehow, his father's face appeared older when he was asleep. His stern jaw was softer, his piercing eyes closed.

Meeting him now, Hawkins thought wryly, *you might mistake him for a kindly middle-aged man. Watch him at the front of his church, pounding his fist on top of the pulpit, and you'd see him for who he really is.*

A warrior of God.

It was a challenge, being the son of a warrior. Personally, Hawkins tended to see shades of gray where his father only saw black and white. He was willing to

216

seek compromise in areas where his father demanded a fight.

Was this a good thing or a bad thing? Would a softer viewpoint help him when he became a preacher? Would it hurt him?

Or would it only leave him confused?

The wagon's headlights flashed over a roadside sign: *Gas and Services 10 miles*. At the bottom of the sign was the logo for Ashfork Big Burger.

"Now we're talking," Hawkins said, letting his fingers dance over the curve of the steering wheel.

24-hour a day fast food. A cheeseburger and chili fries for breakfast. What could be better than that?

But, first, let's hope the bathroom door isn't locked.

* * *

Her hands on her hips, Mrs. Norton kept the tips of her polished shoes a safe distance from the blood encircling Sheriff Archer's head. "Such a bother."

Mr. Brass squatted down to examine the victim's destroyed skull. "I knew Mr. Locke was stupid. Didn't think he was this stupid."

"He was hungry," Alice Poe said.

"Bring him to me," Mrs. Norton said.

"He's gone. He ran off."

"Did he?"

"He killed bad meat," Miss Sweet said. "It would have happened, sooner or later. He always thought he was more than he is."

"And now?" Mr. Brass asked, grinning.

217

"He has a better understanding of his place in the universe."

"This won't do," Mrs. Norton said. "Diseased or not, this was the town's most important law officer. When a policeman disappears, alarms are sounded. People come from everywhere. They scurry about, poking and prying into every corner." She frowned disapprovingly at the corpse. "Did the Sheriff tell anyone he was coming here?"

"I didn't think to ask," Miss Sweet said. "I had no reason."

"Did he have family? A significant other?"

"His heart was empty."

Mr. Brass trailed a finger through the thickening blood. "So, we have a little time." He admired the vibrant color as it drooled down his hand in a winding streak.

Mrs. Norton focused on Alice Poe. "You asked for Mr. Locke. When I allowed you to approach the Void with me, we heard a thousand crying voices. You wanted him."

"I was drawn to him."

"She told him to run," Miss Sweet said.

Alice Poe dropped her eyes, studying the floor. "I could have left. He asked me to go."

"You could have gone. No one keeps any of you here. Did you think of leaving?"

Alice Poe gave a shake of her head.

"I thought as much," Mrs. Norton said. "Return to your room and close the drapes. Find something to put in your mouth. With the sun rising, there may be people on the sidewalk. Your screams must not be heard outside of this building."

"What's to happen with Mr. Locke?" Miss Sweet asked.

Her gaze steady, Mrs. Norton said, "When the Fates decide, we'll meet again."

Mr. Brass nudged the shattered skull in front of him. "What should I do with this?"

"Chop it up. Chop it all up."

* * *

From somewhere in the darkness, she heard a voice. "Liz. Liz Wheeler. Liz, wake up!"

Blinking her eyes, Liz saw Dr. Silva's face in front of her. This close, the pores in his nose were *huge*. "What?"

"You fell asleep in your chair," Dr. Silva said.

Tell me something I don't know, Liz thought. It was amazing she'd stayed awake as long as she had.

The teacher remained inches away from her, an obvious non-believer in the concept of 'personal space'. Liz asked, "Did I miss something important? Are we doing test questions or something?"

"There are still a few hours until the final exam. To get everybody in the right spirit, we're going to play a game."

"A game? Sure, yeah. I'm up for it. Whatever."

"It's my own invention." Dr. Silva smiled. "Calculus Pictionary."

Liz laughed. When his expression fell, she said, "You're serious?"

Past him, the other students were squeezed together on the large sofa. In front of the coffee table, a makeshift

219

easel was positioned. A large sketch pad sat on the lip of the easel, a circle drawn at its center. Inside the circle was an inscribed hexagon.

"What do you think?" Dr. Silva asked.

I am so going to flunk this class, Liz thought. "Great," she said.

* * *

Hawkins guided the car into the parking space labeled *Pastor Parking Only!*

Lost in thought, his father remained in the seat beside him. An hour out of the city, he'd woken abruptly. Other than to ask when they'd arrive in Winterhaven, he hadn't offered any conversation.

Probably another bad dream, Hawkins thought.

His mother had died years ago but his father still awoke with a cry at least twice a month. He was unusually quiet more often than that. Whatever he'd seen while asleep, he kept it to himself. The Reverend wasn't one to share his miseries.

Maybe it wouldn't be such a bad idea for his father to find a new love. It might open him up a little.

Walking together under the darkening clouds, they went through the building's side entrance and into its main classroom. True to their respective natures, Jolene and Jewell had everything ready for the study session.

Seated side by side were five elderly women, one ancient man, and Brenda Parkes, the divorcee who had caught his father's interest. As one, they rose to their feet when Hawkins and the Reverend entered the room. Sloppily but enthusiastically, they applauded.

"Well?" the tiny, gray-haired Jolene asked.

"Did you get into Oklahoma Trinity?" the tiny, white-haired Jewell questioned.

Hawkins blushed. They applauded again.

"Congratulations," Brenda said with a smile. When the others broke into conversation, she moved toward his father.

Reverend Hawkins ignored her. She stopped abruptly before awkwardly returning to her plastic chair.

Going to the window, the Reverend opened the checkerboard curtains. "It's started to rain," he said. "Kristin is here."

Streaks of dirt ran down the glass in rivulets. "Fantastic."

"She's out at the curb. Sitting in a car."

"She didn't come all the way here to wait in the car," Hawkins said. "I'll bet I can get her to come in. Maybe she'll stay for the class."

"No."

"I'm not going to freeze up, Dad. Not that anyone would care if I did, anyway. Kristin certainly won't care."

"That's not what I meant." His face drawn, he let the curtain fall. "Tell her to go. I want her to leave."

"Howard?" Brenda asked, concerned.

Around them, the soft murmur of conversation stopped. Jolene adjusted her hearing aid, wanting to catch every word.

"She doesn't belong here," Reverend Hawkins said. "Something's wrong. I don't know what, but something."

"Dad —"

"Don't let her into the church!"

* * *

Kristin tried Hawkins' cell phone number but, as before, a mechanical voice immediately directed her to a message box. She dropped the phone into her purse.

Overhead, rain drummed against the car's metal roof.

Great, no umbrella, she thought. *And here I am in shorts, a tee and an old sweatshirt.*

When I go up the walk, I'll get soaking wet. Talk about inappropriate attire for your first official visit to church.

She flicked her finger at the dashboard Mickey Mouse. It bobbled to and fro. "It's only a damned building," she told the plastic figure.

Oops, not allowed to say those kinds of things.

That was part of the problem; there were so many rules to be followed. There were things you shouldn't say, things you should say, things you weren't allowed to do, and things you should never, ever, even *think* of doing. If you weren't raised on the Word, you practically needed to consult a play book before even entering the premises.

Not a play book, a Bible. Not that she had one of those lying around, either.

It wasn't like Hawkins hadn't left a dozen of the things at her house. Every few months, she was dropping another one into the donation bin outside the local Salvation Army. She'd actually tried to read one of them, a St. James version of the Old Testament. She hadn't lasted an hour before getting lost in the arcane wording. She felt overwhelmed by all of the begatting and forbading, the "thou this" and the "sayeth that".

222

If the writing of the Bible had been guided by the hand of God, why was it harder to understand than a Stephen King novel? The whole thing was silly. Church, the Bible, religion itself. All of it.

No, be honest with yourself, she thought. *You don't think this is silly. If it were silly, it wouldn't matter.*

The fact is, you're scared.

This wasn't the first time, either. Far from it. Every time she walked past a place of worship, her heart beat like crazy. When Aunt Lois sent her a gold crucifix necklace, it left a welt at the center of her chest. The one time she'd tried to attend Galilee Church, as a birthday surprise for Hawkins, she'd gotten dizzy when she stepped onto its walkway. Feeling sick, she ran back home.

Hawkins still didn't know. What would she have said? "I meant to drop by but I was too busy hurling into the bushes"?

"Not my fault, Hawk," she said. "I tried. Believe it or not, I have a phobia about the whole thing. As if I wasn't damaged enough already."

The condition was called ecclesiophobia, a fear of churches, and she didn't believe there was any such thing, either, until it swept over her. Her favorite on-line encyclopedia said thousands of people suffered from it. She knew Hawkins might doubt her but could he doubt Wikipedia?

"Bet there aren't too many celebrity telethons for this kind of disease," she told Mickey. "Maybe I can form a support group. I'll bet most of us would be free on Sundays."

Mickey's happy expression suggested he liked the idea.

Muffled music played inside her purse. Removing her cell phone, Kristin brought it to her ear.

Before she could say anything, her mother snapped at her. "Where's my car?"

"I have it."

"You asked to borrow it – when?"

Kristin sat in silence. Rain pounded on the roof overhead.

"You're busted, Ms. Grand Theft Auto," Becky continued. "As of this second, the car is off-limits. You want to use it, you'll need written permission."

"Seriously?"

"Yes! No. No, not seriously. Where are you?"

"Galilee Church."

"Pull the other one."

"Hawkins is inside, teaching some kind of study class," Kristin said. "I'm supposed to meet him here."

"You really meant it? Wow." Her mother was quiet for a moment. "How long will you be there?"

"It might be a while." True enough. She'd spent the last ten minutes trying to find the courage to open the car door.

"Make it a short while," Becky said. "We have visitors coming over. I need you to pick up donuts or cinnamon rolls on the way home. Or do you think we should go healthy?"

"Who's visiting?"

"Mrs. Norton. Martin is tagging along, I think."

Kristin's mind spun, her thoughts a jumble.

From somewhere in cyberspace, a crackle rolled over the line. "That was thunder, wasn't it? We'll have lightning soon."

She said, "Mom, I don't feel good about Mrs. Norton."

"She's not very warm and fuzzy, that's for certain. Hang up the line. It's dangerous to be on a phone during a thunderstorm."

"Mrs. Norton –"

"– will need something to eat once she gets here. Martin will, anyway. He's skin and bones since Chandra left him. Pick up something before you get home. A veggie platter!"

The phone line went dead.

Overhead, the rain fell more heavily. Unconcerned, Mickey swayed on his coiled spring leg.

I've got to do this, she told herself. *I have to do it right now.*

Pellets of cold water spat at her legs as she climbed from her seat. Before she could close the car door, a gust of wind yanked the handle from her hand and slammed the driver's side shut.

Lightning streaked overhead, followed by a crash of thunder. She ran for the church walk, feeling as if buckets of water were falling upon her.

Drowning is not an option.

She'd never seen the weather turn nasty so quickly. With the wind howling around her, she bent into it, marveling at the struggle it presented.

At the end of the path, the church's oak door swung open. Hawkins appeared in the vestibule. "Kristin!"

Her hair pressed wetly against her cheeks. Nausea hit her, suddenly, and she gagged dryly.

Nice try, ecclesiophobia, but I'm ready for you this time. I skipped supper, didn't eat breakfast. You might make me as sick as hell but I'm not visiting the bushes this time.

Reverend Hawkins stepped behind his son. He pulled on Hawkins' shirt and the younger man stumbled backward.

The Reverend stared out at her, his eyes wide. Hawkins cried out as his father pushed the big door closed.

The door boomed shut as a black shadow passed over the walkway. The shadow was so large and dark that Kristin wondered if an eclipse had occurred. Shielding her eyes from the rain, she looked up at the sky.

Thick, black clouds floated above her. As she watched, the large, thick drops of rain weakened, transforming into a fine mist. The wind continued to blow but its ferocity was gone. It caressed her, tugging at her clothing.

Wiping the hair from her eyes, she realized she was standing at the doorway of the Galilee Church. She'd been so distracted by the events around her, she'd almost forgotten her fear of the structure itself.

Hawkins shouted something loud and angry from inside the building, only to be answered by his father's deeper, more commanding, voice. Silence followed whatever had been said.

Kristin reached for the door's curved handle. As she touched it, there was a sizzling noise and a searing pain licked across her palm. Crying out, she yanked her fingers away.

A bright red stripe marked where the skin had met the metal handle. Blood bubbled up from the burn line, dripping from the wound and running down her wrist.

"Hawkins!" With her uninjured hand, she banged her fist against the closed door. She pounded her fist again, hearing the sound echo inside the church. "Help me!"

The door remained closed.

Chapter Thirty

Paying for her cup of coffee, Liz wondered, *Why is so much of a life a good news/bad news kind of proposition?*

The good news was, she wasn't going to waste the morning taking a calculus test. The bad news was, she wouldn't graduate from high school, get into the university, or ever qualify for a decent job. In time, she'd end up homeless and begging at street corners for change.

Plus, and this weighed on her heavily, Nana Beggio was going to kill her.

The good news was, she was about to enjoy a fresh cup of half-caff. The bad news was, she was officially broke.

Good news: It had stopped raining. Bad news: If it hadn't stopped raining, she might not have snuck out of Dr. Silva's rear kitchen door and run for freedom. She might even have taken his stupid test.

She wouldn't have *passed* the test, she wasn't kidding herself, but she'd have been present and accounted for. However, important side note, she wasn't entirely to blame for her escape. It was Dr. Silva who uttered the words, "Calculus Pictionary".

My God, she thought, *what kind of warped mind considered joining those two concepts? Calculus Pictionary is worse than it sounds and it sounds like Zombie Death. It's Chinese water torture with math symbols. Drip, quadrant, drip, intercept, drip, Cartesian coordinates.*

It's inhuman, that's what it is. Taken in that light, I should actually be admired for taking a stand and running for daylight.

She sipped at the coffee. Nana Beggio had warned her, if she didn't pass the test and get into Ashfork U., she'd have to find some kind of employment, no matter how menial.

"Completely right and fair, Nana." She raised the coffee cup to the corner stop sign.

Bad news: She lacked any kind of job skills. Good news: Nobody was hiring, anyway.

Opening her cell phone, she saw a blank screen. Bad news: The battery was dead. Worse news: She'd spent the last of her money on hot water and coffee beans.

Worser news: It was a helluva long way home.

She wondered if any of the nearby business owners would let her make a phone call. If so, it wouldn't be those cheap bastards at the coffee shop. They wouldn't even stock toilet paper in their unisex bathroom.

Her eyes searching the stores around her, she spotted a brown tabby walking along the sidewalk ahead of her. "Mouser?"

Mouser ignored her call, his tail twitching as he strolled down the boulevard. Liz grabbed him, spilling splashes of coffee as she picked him up.

"You are in such trouble, mister," she told the cat, not caring about the coffee stains decorating her Elena Garcia blouse.

In her arms, she held the meowing return of her allowance. It was as good as in the bank. Her escape from

229

the Silva Combine wouldn't be forgotten but much would be forgiven.

Because, as incredible as it sounded, Nana Beggio loved this useless cat. She let him sleep on her bed. She wouldn't care –

– how *rancid* he smelled. Crinkling her nose, Liz lowered the animal from her chest. "What did you get into?"

Behind her, a horn blurted loudly. Held loosely, the cat leapt from her hold, jarring the coffee cup from her hand. Liz jumped as steaming liquid sprayed the sidewalk at her feet.

Mouser ran across the street before disappearing over a chain link fence. Liz spun around angrily.

Behind her, a dusty white Chevrolet idled in the center of the street. The car's driver was obscured behind streaks of dirt crisscrossing the windshield.

Walking to the driver's open side window, Liz said, "Were you born a dick?"

"Watch your mouth, girl," the driver told her. "I wasn't *born*."

He was in his twenties and handsome in an arrogant, full-of-himself kind of way. Normally, Liz liked a little attitude in a guy. With this one, she wasn't so sure. "What's your name?"

"Mr. Locke."

"Oh, like I'm going to call you 'mister'." There were reddish-brown splotches on his shirt and pants.

Probably some kind of wood stain, she thought, *which is vaguely sexy if you're into handymen. Which, on reflection, I absolutely am.*

230

He seemed familiar to her but, then, so did the car. "Isn't this Barry Collison's car?"

"Was. I put him in the trunk."

"Not funny." She noticed a hand-lettered FOR SALE sign taped to the car's rear window. She wondered if Barry had bothered to tell this guy that his car had leaked oil on every driveway in town.

"You know the brown-haired girl, right?" Mr. Locke asked. "The snoop, the one who hangs out at the café."

"That's where I've seen you. You work there."

"You know her. The brown-haired girl."

"If you mean, Kristin Faraday," Liz said, "then maybe."

Grimacing, Mr. Locke sagged against the driver's door. Sweat beading his forehead, he thrust an envelope through the open window. "Give her this."

He jerked with pain and the packet fell from his fingers. Striking the ground with a slap, it rested on the street.

Across the front of it, in block letters, he'd written the word, CONFIDENTIAL. A brown fingerprint was imprinted where a stamp would normally be.

Liz pirouetted away from the car. "See ya."

"Wait!" Then, as if the word was foreign to him, he added, "Please."

She stopped at the curb.

"You want money?" He held a pair of bills out to her. When she didn't move, he let the money drop to the asphalt. "That's for you. Just give the brown-haired girl the envelope."

231

A crumpled fifty-dollar bill stared up at her. Folded in beside it was a twenty, a pink smear discoloring Andrew Jackson's image.

"That's a fairly serious bribe for such a small favor."

He put both of his hands on the steering wheel. "The envelope's for your friend, not you. You're not to open it."

Liz shrugged. Behind the car, a pick-up truck blew its horn.

"Give me your promise," Mr. Locke said. "I want to see you swear it."

"It says 'confidential'. I get it, it's none of my business."

The pick-up truck's driver blared his horn a second time. Mr. Locke gunned the car's motor, sending hot air from the engine and sucking the paper bills beneath the Chevy. He drove off, tires squealing, as Liz went into the street for the money.

The truck's driver glared at her as she collected the cash and the stranger's oh-so-important secret message. The truck swerved around her, its horn beeping.

She flipped her middle finger into the air then looked for the handyman. Barry Collison's car had vanished.

Ripping open the tip of the envelope, Liz found two sheets of paper. Unfolding the top sheet, she started to read it.

Halfway through the first page, she began to laugh.

* * *

232

Miss Sweet entered the bedroom. Unmoving, Alice Poe lay atop her bed's bare mattress, her eyes pointed at the ceiling above her.

A star burst of cracks was visible on her upper left shoulder. Through the cloud of her body, Miss Sweet could see similar markings on her torso and upper legs.

Mrs. Norton had been exceptionally angry this time.

"I've packed our belongings," Miss Sweet prompted.

"You haven't taken my things."

"It won't take long. You don't have much."

"I have a little doll. Did I show it to you?" Alice Poe rolled onto her side, facing the seer. "It has the biggest eyes and the smallest mouth. Because I'm so quiet."

"You keep a toy?"

"Mr. Locke gave it to me." Sitting up, she rested her hands on her knees. "I know he thinks his gift didn't mean anything."

"What do you think?"

Alice Poe touched a sad finger to her lips.

"I can't do this alone," Miss Sweet said. "Get dressed and we'll carry the boxes downstairs."

"What about the Other?"

"What of her?"

"I wish she wasn't here. I wish we'd left, the instant we saw her."

"Mrs. Norton will take care of it."

"What if she doesn't? What if she can't?" Alice Poe hugged herself. "It was foolish to return here. It was arrogant."

"I don't remember you sharing such thoughts before."

233

"It's the Dark Ones who empower Mrs. Norton. They give her the ability to do the things she does. Sometimes I wonder if she forgets who she serves."

"Never," Miss Sweet assured her.

"She should have been more careful. She was greedy."

"What good is a power if you don't use it?" Miss Sweet asked. "You worry too much about the girl."

"Because no one else worries about her at all!"

"Mrs. Norton has a plan."

"It will fail, it will fail." Still hugging herself, Alice Poe rocked gently. "If I had blood, I'd feed it to your stone. Then you'd see."

In irritation, Miss Sweet banged the foot of her cane against the floor. "This is nonsense."

"I had a vision."

"A vision?" Miss Sweet's hand froze, her cane dangling in the air. "Do you mean, a dream?"

Alice Poe continued rocking silently.

"Don't talk to me of such things. We don't dream."

"Did my lips disappear? Did you see me say something not true?" Alice Poe raised her head. "Don't ask me to go with you. I can do what I want. Mrs. Norton said no one keeps us here."

"She never thought you would consider it."

"She *said*." Alice Poe's bare feet touched the floor. Overhead, the light shimmered, accenting the star bursts decorating her body.

Miss Sweet said, "Mrs. Norton will find Mr. Locke, you know. There will be punishment."

"I'd be with him now if he wanted me," Alice Poe said. "If he'd ever for a second shown he wanted me." She went to her closet.

"How will you feed?" Miss Sweet rubbed her hand over the head of her cane. "There's so much bad meat."

Buttoning her blouse, Alice Poe said, "You could tell me who to choose."

"How?" As the realization dawned, she said, "The two of us?"

"Why not?"

"Mrs. Norton would be angry."

"She gave us permission. She said we could leave."

"Yes," Miss Sweet said slowly, "perhaps she did."

"We're not doing anything wrong. Not like Mr. Locke. She won't stop until she has him."

"She'll torture him. Year after year. He'll wish he'd never left the Void."

"She'll be too busy to concern herself with us," Alice Poe said soothingly. "She'll remember saying it was our choice to stay or to go. Besides, we'll have left before she returns."

"If she returns. You had a vision."

"Yes, I did." Alice Poe's mouth remained as true as ever.

"There would be no one to tell us what to do if Mrs. Norton was gone," Miss Sweet said.

"No one to punish us."

"We could feed when we wanted."

"We wouldn't have to wait. We could both feed on the same night."

"Who would suspect the two of us? A fragile young thing and her crippled grandmother?"

235

Alice Poe said, "No one."

"Let me think about it," Miss Sweet told her, "while you get the rest of our things ready."

* * *

Her mother was waiting at the door when she arrived home.

"At last," Becky said. "They're not here yet. What did you get?"

Kristin shook her head.

"You couldn't stop for a box of donuts? It would have taken five minutes." For the first time, she noticed the t-shirt wrapped around Kristin's hand. Her tone softened. "What happened?"

"I don't know."

Becky touched a finger to a stain on the shirt. "You're bleeding, honey."

"A little."

"Are you hurt? Was there an accident?"

"Mom, it's a couple of scratches. I'll get the first aid kit." Kristin ran up the stairs.

From below, Becky said, "Put Betadine on it!"

Kristin locked the bathroom door. Unwrapping the t-shirt, she examined her hand.

An angry line ran through the center of her palm. It throbbed hotly, leaking blood as she watched. She pressed a nail to her injured flesh, trying to examine the skin, and almost cried out from the pain.

A bad burn, that's all, she thought. *There's no tear in the skin, no puncture site.*

A red pool formed slowly in her cupped hand.

Can burns cause you to bleed? I've watched a thousand medical shows, I've never seen anybody bleeding from their burns.

Rinsing her hand, she squirted aloe vera ointment at the center of the wound. Under the sink, she found a roll of gauze and wrapped it tightly around her palm. Taping the dressing closed, she grabbed a bottle of ibuprofen tablets from the medicine cabinets.

"Better make it a double, bartender," she told her image in the mirror, "it's been a hard day." Filling her mouth with water from the faucet, she swallowed the pills.

"Now what?" she asked her image.

She'd read somewhere, someone wasn't truly paranoid if people were really out to get them. She wondered if what she had could be truly called 'ecclesiophobia' when it was obvious the church was truly out to get her.

Using her cell phone, she dialed Hawkins number. The call went to voice mail on the first ring.

Downstairs, the doorbell sounded. She heard the door open and voices rise in conversation.

"Maybe you should sit this one out," she told her reflection. "I don't think you're up to dealing with Mrs. Norton right now."

"Kristin!" her mother called. "Could you come down here please?"

She closed the medicine cabinet.

Downstairs, her mother sat in the easy chair. On the sofa, sitting side by side, was Mrs. Norton, Martin Piotrowski and the horribly-solid Mr. Brass.

"Mom?"

237

Becky smiled at her as she entered the room. "Hand all better?"

Concerned, Mr. Brass said, "You hurt?"

"Was it a cut?" Mrs. Norton asked.

"It's nothing." Kristin tucked her hand behind her.

"We should go," Mr. Brass said, rising from his seat. Mrs. Norton put a hand on his shoulder. As if he was being pressed under a heavy weight, he dropped back down.

"Please stay," Becky said. "The kettle is on. Besides, you haven't given Kristin her present."

"We wouldn't want to leave until we've done that," Mrs. Norton said.

Kristin couldn't imagine what kind of present would be offered by the likes of these two. *A rat infested with the bubonic plague? A rabid skunk?*

"We can spare a few more minutes," Mrs. Norton told her companion.

"Take a chair, honey," her mother said. "Have you met Mr. Brass?"

"I know him." At the tone of her voice, her mother looked at her sharply. Pretending she hadn't noticed, Kristin went to the recliner.

"I probably shouldn't have come," Martin said.

"You're right." Mrs. Norton patted his knee. "We'd prefer to be without you, dear heart, but you made such a scene. When you stopped us in the street, you practically crawled through the car window to join us."

When the tea kettle whistled, Becky left the room to answer it.

Martin's cheeks flushed. "I didn't think you'd mind a little company."

"The truth is, you're lonely. You're interested in me sexually."

Kristin couldn't believe what she'd just heard. She didn't know how to react or what to say.

"Unfortunately, I've never really enjoyed sexual relations," Mrs. Norton said, in a conversational tone. "I find the entire experience a bit hot and unpleasant. So much exertion, so much noise, for so small a reward. If the time comes that I do decide to have sex again, I'll certainly make an effort to find someone more appealing than you."

Quietly, Martin said, "Constance. Please."

"Have I said too much? Been too open? I've only been polite to you, Martin, because I hoped you might prove useful."

The old man paled. "That's – that's not true."

Mrs. Norton's crystal face wrinkled in amusement. "That's what I like about people. When you tell them lies, they believe you. Tell them the truth, they're completely befuddled." Her face smoothed when she considered Kristin. "Everyone except for you."

Becky returned, carrying a serving tray. She raised a knife from the tray. "It's not the freshest pumpkin bread you'll ever eat but it's still tasty. Who wants a slice?"

No one responded.

"Mrs. Norton? Martin?"

"Nothing for me," Mrs. Norton told her. "The best bread is made from scratch. You've used a store brand mix and not an especially good one. The piece I tried was almost as bad as your artwork."

Becky's mouth dropped open. The serrated knife clattered onto the tray.

239

Mrs. Norton said, "I made Mr. Brass come along whenever I wasted time at your gallery. He shares my opinion about your work. He's seen more than enough of your paintings."

"I like your barns," Mr. Brass said.

The tray wobbled in her mother's hands. Becky set it on the coffee table before slumping into the easy chair.

"Isn't this refreshing?" Mrs. Norton told the group. "It's so rare we're allowed to be totally open with your kind. Too often, we have to watch our words."

"We don't like to lie," Mr. Brass explained. His hand dragged over his face. "We don't like how it feels."

Kristin watched as the glass woman opened her purse. "Before we go, I have a little something for your daughter."

Kristin said, "Whatever it is, I don't want it."

Stirring in her chair, Becky said, "You should leave, Mrs. Norton. I want you out of my house."

"Yes." Martin lifted up, his thin body practically vibrating with tension. "Go."

Without leaving his seat, Mr. Brass punched Martin in the stomach. The blow sent the smaller man backwards, spilling over the coffee table. When his arm hit the serving tray, it sent the cups and saucers into the air.

Becky jerked as if she'd been struck.

"I'm calling the police," Kristin said.

"I'd be curious to see if there's anybody to answer the call," Mr. Brass said. Opening his jacket, he brought out a small pistol. "Not all that long ago, we had a pawnshop. When this little Pepperbox derringer came through, I decided to keep it. Tiny, right? Only holds four rounds."

His thumb pulled on the pistol's trigger. When Martin sat up, Mr. Brass aimed the gun at the old man's head. "In most cases, four rounds is plenty."

Mrs. Norton brought a small, white box from her purse. She told Kristin, "Take it."

Chapter Thirty-One

Wouldn't you know, Liz thought, *it has to be Sam Bolland who picks me up.*

In her junior year, she'd been Sam's lab partner in A&P. Sam dropped out of Anatomy and Physiology – and high school itself – in mid-semester, just before exams. The general consensus among the teaching staff was that their former student just didn't like to take tests.

Lacking any sort of skills or training, Sam had one advantage in life: He was Tim Fortier's nephew. While his uncle had never expressed the least amount of admiration for his sister's son, he felt an obligation to give him a job.

So here she was, riding in the back seat of a blue-and-white Tim's Taxi, and staring at the dandruff-flaked, Supercuts-styled hair of her former classmate. She couldn't help but wonder if this was merely a coincidence or if she was to view his appearance as some apocalyptic glimpse into the future that lay ahead of her.

In short, did Sam's present lifestyle, clearly affected by the absence of a high school diploma, somehow represent Liz Wheeler's future? Was he her own personal vision of Dickens' Christmas Yet to Come?

God, I hope not.

"Men's courses will foreshadow certain ends," she quoted out loud. "But if the courses be departed from, the ends will change. Say it is thus with what you show me!"

Sam punched at the buttons of the dashboard radio. "What did you say?"

"Quoting a book I read."

"Yeah," he said, as if he wasn't certain of this foreign word, 'book'. He cranked the radio knob, raising its volume.

Twist the knob a bit more, Sam, Liz thought. *Country music is best when it's loud. The way things stand, I can still hear myself think.*

Think about not getting into college and realize I don't care, not the way I should. Think about my future and discover, somehow, I'm already bored.

All things considered, I'd rather turn off the old brainpan. That okay with you?

She straightened when the car rolled past a broken-down Hyundai at the side of the road. The car's hood was up and its owner was hunched over the engine.

"Stop the taxi!"

Sam turned off the radio. "What?"

"Stop the car, Sam. Right here. Now!"

Obediently, he hit the brakes. Opening the taxi's passenger door, Liz ran to the Hyundai.

Hawkins was scratching at his head when she peered at him from under the hood. "Want a lift?"

He glanced over at her. "Third time it's broken down this year. I just replaced the radiator, too."

"Sorry."

"This car is such a POS."

"What've I been telling you?"

"Let it go, Liz," Hawkins said. "I need to talk to Kristin. Not by texting, not over a phone, but in person. Friend-to-friend."

243

"You've got issues?"

"Maybe." He scratched at his head. "I honestly don't know."

"I was on my way to her place." Liz gestured at the taxi in the center of the street. "You can hitch a ride."

"My father doesn't want me to see her. He practically begged me to stay with him."

"Some church thing?"

"No. Dad had a nightmare and now he's scared of Kristin."

"Get out," Liz said. There wasn't the slightest trace of humor in Hawkins' face. "Our Kristin?"

In the gloomiest voice she'd ever heard, he said, "He says she's Satan's spawn."

Linking her arm with his, she led him to the taxicab.

"Normally, the deranged Dad thing would really pique my interest," Liz said, "but wait 'til you hear about my day."

* * *

Taking the container, Kristin cradled it in her gauze-wrapped hand. Curled across the lid, gold lettering read, *Ashfork Imports and Oddities.*

"Too late for the job now, I'm afraid," Mrs. Norton said. "I doubt it would have worked out, anyway. They were seeking an assistant with a little discretion."

Nestled inside the box were three brown capsules. Kristin picked up the center pill to examine it. "It's filled with dirt."

"Dirt? No. It's Hyoscyamus niger. Henbane." She frowned. "What's the matter with you, child? Didn't you ever read Hamlet?"

"In Sophomore English."

"Well?"

Kristin shook her head.

"It's poison."

Becky rose from her chair. "Poison!"

Mr. Brass shifted his weapon, pointing the pistol at Becky. "Sit."

"Fetch a glass of water," Mrs. Norton said. "You'll need it to swallow the pills."

Kristin spilled the tablet into its box. "You first."

"You can't be serious," Martin said to Mrs. Norton as he climbed to his knees. "That's insane."

"Name-calling, Martin?"

"My daughter is not taking those pills," Becky said. "Martin's right. The two of you need help."

"I told you to sit down." Mr. Brass pointed the mouth of the derringer at Becky's forehead. "Do it now, meat."

"Fuck you."

Stepping over the corner of the end table, Mr. Brass cocked his arm. When Becky started to speak, he swung his fist out, smashing his gun hand against the side of her head. She crumpled, her eyes glazing as her legs collapsed.

"Mom!" Kristin cried as her mother slid from the white seat cushion and fell to the ground.

Mr. Brass examined his victim. "Still breathing. Might have lost a tooth or two but she's okay."

"You hurt her!"

245

"Could have been worse."

He straightened as Martin sprang forward. *"Die!"* the old man cried.

Holding the recovered bread knife, he plunged the weapon into his enemy's chest. The knife protruding from his shirt, Mr. Brass staggered under the blow. His knees shook and his legs trembled.

Then, giving a laugh, he straightened. He grinned at Martin. "I really had you going."

Pointing the derringer at his assailant, he pulled its trigger. The gun barked and Martin screamed. Clutching at his leg, he fell to the floor.

"Mr. Piotrowski!" Kristin stopped short when Mr. Brass pressed the gun to her chest.

"He stabs me so he thinks he killed me," Mr. Brass said, his eyes bright. "Man, oh man, you should have seen the look on his face."

Kristin thought, *If I could kill* you*, I would.*

She'd never been so angry. Her right hand throbbed, pulsing with each beat of her heart. Glancing at her wrapped hand, she saw a pinpoint of color growing in the center of the gauze.

His hands clutching his leg, Martin rolled on the ground. Blood leaked from inside his trousers, spreading through his interlocked fingers.

Yanking the knife from his chest, Mr. Brass tossed it to the floor. "One of life's special moments, you know what I mean?"

Dipping a hand into his pocket, he removed a bullet. Smoothly, he reloaded the gun.

There was a knock at the front door.

"Too much commotion," Mrs. Norton said softly. "Noise attracts attention." Facing Kristin, she whispered, "Call out, say anything, and your mother dies."

The front door handle rattled. "Anybody home?"

It was Liz's voice. Kristin held her breath.

"Everyone be quiet," Mrs. Norton said. "People leave when a house appears empty."

Martin moaned, earning himself a reprimanding glance from Mrs. Norton. He curled into a fetal position as the carpet darkened beneath him.

From outside, Hawkins said, "Don't have a heart attack, Lizzer."

A shuffle of footsteps was followed by the sound of metal meeting metal. To Kristin's horror, the lock turned and the door opened.

"I house sit sometimes," Hawkins explained over his shoulder as he entered. "I've had a key for a couple of years."

"I should have worn a sweater," Liz said, following behind him. "Kristin's mom pumps the air conditioner like crazy. It's always like a morgue...."

The pair stopped at the sight in front of them. Mr. Brass gestured with his gun hand.

"Shut the door," Mrs. Norton said. After Liz did, she asked the pair, "Did anyone come with you? Is there someone waiting outside?"

"She'll know if you're lying," Kristin told them.

Hawkins looked at her, puzzled.

"We took a cab," Liz said. "The driver left before Hawkins reached the curb."

"Mister Piotrowski?" Hawkins said. "He's bleeding!" Then, seeing the unconscious Becky on the floor, he said, "Shit."

"Nobody has to die," Mr. Brass told them. "Not yet, anyway. The two of you stand over there, across from the front window."

"Kristin?"

"Do it, Hawk," she said. Obediently, her friends retreated to the corner of the room.

"If you'd done as I'd asked," Mrs. Norton said to Kristin, "if you'd taken the Henbane, we'd be gone by now."

"Henbane," Liz said, alarmed.

"What?"

"Henbane is a poison."

"What's going on?" Hawkins asked Kristin.

"I wish I knew."

"If you're concerned for your friends," Mrs. Norton said, "if you care for your mother, you'll do as I ask."

Kristin considered the capsules in the box. Clear gelatin shells containing a mocha interior, they didn't seem like much. *Isn't poison marked with a skull and crossbones?*

She replaced the lid. "Never."

"Never is such a long time." To Mr. Brass, Mrs. Norton asked, "You have more bullets if I need them?"

"Always be prepared, that's my motto. Me and the scouts," Mr. Brass said.

"More bullets?" Hawkins said. "Why would you need more bullets?"

Mr. Brass chuckled.

"Miss Sweet never met this pair," Mrs. Norton warned her subordinate. "We know nothing about their future. They appear to be healthy but you can't know about young people. Sometimes it's not the body that's the problem."

"I could put a slug in the boy."

Mrs. Norton reflected on the idea. "Not a killing shot, you understand. Aim for the stomach."

Mr. Brass thumbed the derringer's trigger. Hawkins tensed, his body growing rigid.

"Don't," Kristin said, moving in front of him. "He's not part of this. He didn't do anything."

"I could do the girl instead, you want," Mr. Brass told her. "As a favor."

Kristin said, "If you're going to shoot anyone, shoot me." She stepped closer, her chest nearly touching the gun's barrel.

"There's an idea," Mr. Brass said. He let his arm drop.

"He can't," Liz said from the corner. "He's not allowed to hurt you. Neither of them can hurt you."

Mrs. Norton grew very still.

Liz swallowed nervously. "There was this creep in a car, Kristin. This Mr. Locke. He wrote you a letter."

Uneasily, Mr. Brass shifted his weight from one leg to the other. His gun continued to point at the floor.

"The letter was all about his family," Liz said. "Mrs. Norton and the others, the ones working at the café. He called them, 'the Unending'." Apologetically, she added, "I thought it was a joke."

"What else did he write?" Mrs. Norton asked.

"You have rules." Liz's voice grew fainter. "You did – something – to Kristin and, now, you can't harm her. Your masters won't allow it."

"They haven't touched me, Liz," Kristin said. "During the time they've been here, all the time they've been in Winterhaven, they haven't done anything to me."

Liz dropped her gaze.

"What is it?" she asked.

Liz didn't answer, shaking her head.

She knows, Kristin thought. *Whatever they're supposed to have done, Liz has the answer. It was in the letter. The letter she thought was a joke.*

But look at Mr. Brass. Look at Mrs. Norton. They don't think it's funny.

"Mr. Locke, ever an embarrassment," Mrs. Norton said. To Liz, she added, "Where is the letter he gave you?"

"Are you people listening to yourselves?" Hawkins asked. "To the words you're saying? You need help."

Shrugging the shoulder strap from her arm, Liz opened her purse. Removing a sheet of paper, she crumpled the page into a ball and threw it at her captors' feet.

Mrs. Norton collected the piece of paper. She smoothed it flat, reading the writing in front of her.

"Printed letters, poor spelling, betrayal in every sentence," she said. "It's not even signed. Whatever shall I do with him?"

"Can we go?" Mr. Brass asked. "I think we should leave."

"Mr. Locke shared a few of our secrets," she told him. "Not all of them. Not the most important ones." She

250

folded the sheet, putting it in her handbag. "We'll wait a bit longer."

"Don't waste your time," Kristin said. "If I took the Henbane, you'd kill everyone, anyway."

Mrs. Norton said, "The people here mean nothing to me. Less than nothing. True, yes? You can see?"

Her mouth remained unchanged.

"Do as I ask and no one else gets hurt," she said. "We'll leave and they'll never see either of us again."

"What about you?" Kristin asked Mr. Brass.

"I do what she tells me. Not that I wouldn't mind seeing things end differently."

Then it struck her. She finally understood what they wanted and why they wanted it. With a stammer in her voice, she said, "You w-want to *absorb* me."

"Goodness, no." Mrs. Norton laughed lightly. "Whatever gave you that idea? You'd have no more flavor than a dry biscuit."

"She's already tasted you," Mr. Brass said.

"I couldn't resist," Mrs. Norton said. "Your soul was so young, so pure. Delicious."

"Her *soul*?" Hawkins asked.

"Gone now, of course."

She's not lying, Kristin realized. *She actually believes this. From the expression on Mr. Brass' face, he believes it, too.*

Where's Dr. Ron when you really need him?

Hawkins said, "Gone? What does that mean, 'gone'?"

"They think she ate Kristin's soul," Liz explained. "That's what she told Mr. Locke, anyway. That's what he put in the letter."

Hawkins' lips parted but he didn't say anything. Closing his eyes, he lowered his head. His mouth moved silently.

Pray if you think it'll help, Hawk. Kristin said, "You can't take a soul. No one can do that."

"Your ignorance no longer astounds me, girl," Mrs. Norton replied. "Besides, you got as much as you gave. Marvelous gifts. Powers, really. Not that I expected you to keep them." She gave the tiniest of shrugs. "I'm disappointed with the people in your life. When you were a baby, they should have sensed you didn't belong. You never should have been allowed to live."

"You're not one of them," Mr. Brass indicated Liz and Hawkins, "you're not one of us. A little bit of dust, that's all you are."

Mrs. Norton said, "You're an Other, dear. You belong with no one; you never will. Quit fighting the inevitable and accept your place. End this."

Her hand throbbing, Kristin raised the lid of the box. Hawkins' eyes snapped open. "Don't take the pills!"

Mr. Brass pointed the derringer at him.

"It's just...." Hawkins let the sentence fade. "It's a sin," he said, trying again. "A mortal sin. There's no chance of repentance."

"Yeah?" Mr. Brass said, interested. "You think so?"

A rattling sound gasped up from their feet. Kristin said, "Mister Piotrowski?"

The carpet around the old man was the color of rust. His head lolled back and his mouth fell open.

"An artery," Mrs. Norton said to Mr. Brass, her voice filled with venom. "You hit an *artery*."

252

Martin's lips quivered before he gave a final, wheezing exhalation of air.

Mrs. Norton roared in anger, her mouth suddenly huge and filled with sharp, pointed teeth. Shimmering waves rose from Martin Piotrowski's body, looping around her crystal body and flowing down her throat. Mrs. Norton's spine arched and her mouth snapped shut.

Hawkins said, "Did you see? Did you see her teeth?"

Life flowed into Mrs. Norton. Mr. Brass inched away from her, avoiding physical contact.

Hawkins bent to the carpet as Liz crept beside Kristin.

"Listen," Liz whispered, "the creep, that Locke, he wrote a bunch of wild things. More than Mrs. Norton knows. There were two pages to the letter he gave me."

Mrs. Norton took a deep, trembling breath, as her skin turned to pink. Her hair blossomed into view, its tight brown curls fashionably cut.

"I aimed for the old man's leg," Mr. Brass told her. "People don't die from those kinds of shots. They don't die from a bullet in their leg."

Standing, Hawkins held the bread knife. Shielding the weapon from Mrs. Norton's view, he joined his friends.

"I've seen Martin Piotrowski's future," Mrs. Norton said to Mr. Brass, her words tight and mean. "For him, the years to come were sad and lonely. Every day of his misery will be mine, intensified." With satisfaction, she added, "I'll make certain you feel it, too."

Keeping her voice low, Liz said, "Locke wrote there's only one thing capable of stopping his kind. You – your blood – is the only thing that scares them. The only thing that can kill the Unending."

"Take this." Hawkins pushed the knife toward Kristin. "I can't stab anyone. Not even them. Not even now."

Oh, Hawk, Kristin thought, *you believe I can?*

She looked at her mother. A trickle of blood leaked from the corner of Becky's mouth.

Maybe so.

Grasping the knife's handle, Kristin slipped its blade through the waistband of her jeans.

Mrs. Norton's gaze fell on them. "Gathered together, are you? Show some manners, children. Face your guests."

They did as she commanded.

Mrs. Norton said, "The pills."

"Enough with the pills," Hawkins said. As if even he couldn't believe what he was doing, he slapped the box. The tablets flew into the air.

Mrs. Norton started to cry out when an expression of deep sadness transformed her face. Grabbing at Mr. Brass's arm, she pressed her face to his chest.

"Get the poison," she said, her words dissolving into a sob.

The capsules bounced on the floor, separating as they rolled over the tan surface. Liz reached out her foot, slamming a shoe on top of a pair of tablets. They puffed up in a tiny cloud of powder.

"Bye," Liz said.

Mr. Brass swept the remaining pill into his fist. He brought it to Mrs. Norton.

She wiped at her eyes. "One pill left. Only one. Nausea, cramps, vomiting – at best."

"I couldn't stop them," Mr. Brass said. "You were holding my gun arm."

"My fault, then?"

His face fell. "Their fault. I'm saying, this was their fault."

"They must feel quite clever." To Kristin, Mrs. Norton said, "You can see I have color?"

"Yes."

"That's what happens once we're filled," Mrs. Norton said. "We no longer need to eat. We have nearly one full year before we must feed again."

"You do this every year?"

"Then you're done for now," Liz said.

Relieved, Hawkins said, "You've fed. You can leave us alone."

"My, but you're simple things." Mrs. Norton toyed with a curl of her hair, seeming to find pleasure in its touch. "I meant we no longer need to fear we might – what was your word? – 'absorb' bad meat."

Slumped beside the easy chair, Becky moaned softly.

"If your mother had done her job all those years ago, none of us would be in this situation, would we?" Mrs. Norton mused. "The world won't suffer from the loss of yet another bad artist. When we leave here, Mr. Brass, I want you to shoot her in the head."

Kristin gasped.

"But, first," Mrs. Norton said, "finish the boy. The red-haired girl, too."

"Be a pleasure."

255

The blood drained from Hawkins' face. Liz clenched her fists.

Kristin closed her hand over the circle of blood at the center of the gauze. "Why? Why do any of this? You don't have to. You can just leave."

"Left alive, your friends will tell tales, won't they? Someone might decide to listen to them." A considered look came into Mrs. Norton's eyes. "Besides, you've become an irritant. I rather like the idea of you spending the next few years, trying to explain what happened to the local authorities."

"You don't think I'll tell them about you?"

"I'm certain you'll try," Mrs. Norton said. "But will they believe you?"

"Customers tell me you're kind of the town celebrity," Mr. Brass interjected. "One of the downsides of spending time in the nuthouse."

Her hand tightening around the knife's handle, Kristin felt something wet run from under the gauze bandage and down her wrist. *Shouldn't I be scared? Shouldn't I be – like, Hawkins?*

But I'm not like Hawk. Not like Liz.

"As your friend said, there's nothing I can physically do to harm you," Mrs. Norton admitted. "So, we'll improvise. It's not a perfect solution but we'll make it work."

"Just leave," Kristin said, "I beg you. I won't say anything, I won't tell anyone."

"A tempting offer but – no."

Mr. Brass raised the derringer to Kristin's temple. "Love to do you first."

"Go ahead."

"Rules is rules." Shifting the gun, he aimed past her. "Move over a little, I'll give your friends a clean death."

"Mr. Brass," Mrs. Norton said, fear in her words. "Blood."

The big man followed her gaze. Fresh spots of red dotted the carpet at Kristin's feet. When he raised his eyes to the teen's face, she had the knife held above her head.

A streak of blood ran the length of the knife's silver blade.

"Do it," Liz whispered.

Dropping the mouth of his weapon toward Kristin's stomach, Mr. Brass desperately tried to cock his gun. His thumb slipped and the trigger fell to its base harmlessly. He tried again when Mrs. Norton hit him, hard, across the jaw.

"Rules," she said.

He blinked at her, uncertainly, as Kristin thrust the knife into his chest. It sliced into his skin with a familiar sound.

Schhhct!

Mr. Brass staggered under the blade's impact. His knees shook and his legs wobbled. For one terrible second, she thought he was pretending, once again.

His eyes grew bigger. He clutched the knife's handle, only to cry out when his fingers touched a reddish smear. Where he'd touched Kristin's blood, his skin bubbled, turning black.

Mr. Brass screamed. The sound rose and fell, the noise echoing as if it was erupting inside an empty chamber. Victim after victim cried out from inside him, a shrieking cacophony of pain.

The teenagers pressed their hands to their ears. Expressionless, as if she'd heard such screams before, Mrs. Norton crossed the front entry. Without looking back, she exited to the street.

In mid-cry, the remaining member of the Unending pitched forward. Suddenly silent, he hit the floor with a thump, driving the knife to its hilt. Face down on the carpet, he lay motionless.

Cautiously, Kristin lowered her hands from her ears. "Is he dead?"

His body jerked. His limbs writhing, Mr. Brass shifted inside of the oversized blue LL Bean shirt. His skin puckered as it shrank, darkening in color. His legs danced, the feet shrinking from their shoes and disappearing inside the length of the jeans. Even his hair changed, silver growing over gray and black as the head holding it sank below the shirt collar.

The three of them stared at the fallen body.

Liz said, "This is beyond wrong."

Hawkins poked at the back of the shirt. It collapsed, as if the body inside of it was now too small to support the fabric. "Roll him over"

Kristin gripped Mr. Brass' shirt and tugged. When his dead face rolled over to meet them, Kristin, Liz and Hawkins all cried out.

Dressed in the cook's clothing, the cold face of Susannah Guitierrez stared up at them.

"We killed Ms. Guitierrez?" Hawkins cried.

Kristin yanked on the knife and Susannah's body lifted as the blade came free. A cracking noise followed the weapon's escape and she shattered. Her body broke into pieces, like so much caramel-colored marble.

Again, the three teenagers screamed.

The shards holding Susannah's image crumbled. Melting, they left a trail of flesh-colored particles within the abandoned clothing.

Nothing but dust, Kristin thought.

"I'm going to need years of therapy," Liz said. "Years and years of extensive therapy."

Despite her words, she sounded more excited than shocked. Saying nothing, Hawkins' face was pale.

Becky moaned and Kristin hurried over to her. Her mother's eyes blinked open. Her lower lip was split and swollen.

Sounding dazed, Becky said, "Still alive, I guess."

"You okay?"

Alarm pierced the cloud in her mother's eyes. "Where's Mr. Brass?"

"Gone."

"Mrs. Norton?"

"She's gone, too," Hawkins said.

Gone? Kristin thought. *Gone from here, anyway. Gone for now.*

Gone from Winterhaven, too, or will be, soon enough. Escaping with the remainder of her family, the ones at the restaurant. Free to prey on the rest of the world.

Then she decided, *Not if I can help it.*

"Good riddance." Becky's tongue played inside her mouth. "Damn, I think he got one of my molars."

"You need to rest." Hawkins joined her and they helped Becky into her chair.

Becky looked at her daughter. "What is it?"

"I've got to go out."

259

"Now?"

"It's important. I'll come back as soon as I can."

"Not now, honey. Not...I don't want...." Her sentence trailed off. Yawning, Becky closed her eyes.

Kristin told her friends, "Call nine-one-one, okay?"

"No, you don't," Hawkins said. "You heard your mom."

Going into the kitchen, Kristin collected the car keys. When she returned to the living room, Hawkins had his arms crossed over his chest. "No."

"Got no choice, Hawk."

"Why?" When that didn't garner a response, he said, "Where are you going?"

"To find Mrs. Norton," she said.

"Forget it. You'll never catch her."

"This isn't only about her."

"Let's wait for the paramedics. Or the cops."

"Kristin doesn't have time," Liz said. "There are more of those – things – waiting at the café."

"So?"

Kristin raised the knife, still streaked with her blood.

"Oh." Hawkins gathered his thoughts. Taking a deep breath, he opened his cell phone. "What should I tell the ambulance crew?"

His finger paused, hovering over the key pad.

"Blame everything on Mrs. Norton," Kristin said. "Tell them she snapped. Tell them she's evil."

"I can do that."

Liz touched Kristin's arm. "Wait."

God, I wish I could. "I'd love to stay here, Lizzer, you know I would. I just can't."

"I meant wait," Liz told her, "until I get a knife, too."

* * *

The girls had left and Becky was sitting up, sipping tea, by the time Hawkins finished with the Emergency Dispatcher. He had one more call to make and was pleased when his father picked up on the first ring.

"I'm okay, Dad, really," Hawkins said.

His father's sharp response caused the speaker to buzz in his ear. Hawkins responded, "No, not right now."

He checked on Becky. She smiled at him wanly.

"I'll get there when I can," he continued. "I'm kind of in the middle of something right now."

His father replied heatedly. When he stopped speaking, Hawkins could hear Brenda Parkes in the background, trying to soothe him.

Good for her. "I'll be home as soon as I can. Promise."

His father barked again but in a softer, less worried tone.

"Listen, I've got a question for you," Hawkins said. "A Biblical question. I think I know the answer but I want to make sure.

"Do angels have souls?"

Chapter Thirty-Two

From Kristin's Diary

Four blocks away from Piotrowski's Café, we heard the sirens wailing. When the restaurant came into view, I drove Mom's car to the curb.

There were two fire engines flanking the building, their pumpers spraying water. A team of firefighters fought against the power of a long double-jacketed fire hose, directing its stream into the blaze. Even from where we were parked, we could hear water sizzling and hissing as it fell upon the charred skeleton of the restaurant.

"Think it was an accident?" Liz knew it wasn't. After a little bit, she said, "Could be burning for a long time. All of the fryer grease."

A big enough fire, a hot enough burn, and every last bit of Piotrowski's would be cooked. Well, not the stainless-steel equipment or the walk-in freezer, I guess, but everything else. All of the previous owner's personal belongings.

All of the evidence. Any possible clues.

Liz was quiet then, pretending to be interested in my dashboard Mickey Mouse. While she used an emerald nail to poke at Mickey's face, I removed the gauze from around my hand.

There was a crust of dried blood at the center of my palm. When I rubbed my thumb over it, the crust crumbled into flakes. The blood and the burn were gone. My hand appeared completely normal.

"Think anybody was still inside when the fire started?" Liz asked. "One of Mrs. Norton's family?"

"I wish," I told her, and I do, too. Mrs. Norton isn't a person. The things surrounding her, working with her, aren't people, either.

I want them all dead.

"What do we do next?" Liz asked.

"We?"

"Girlfriend," she told me, "hunting monsters *has* to be more fun than Calculus Pictionary."

*

What happens next, Liz? I don't have any idea.

Of course, that's kind of the recurrent theme of my entire life. What do I do next and when should I do it?

I don't know.

Is it possible for someone's soul to be eaten? Do people even *have* souls?

Don't know.

What is Mrs. Norton, really? Where did she come from? How many more of her kind are out there?

Don't know.

Liz can't be serious about the two of us hunting those things. Can she?

Don't know.

Will I ever move from Winterhaven and have a normal life?

Well, that one's probably not such a mystery. I think the 'normal' option disappeared the day I met Dr.

263

Ron. It just took me awhile to realize it. But that doesn't mean I can't have a good life.

Which brings me to a few other things I know.

I intend to keep my writing in my diary. I thought about giving it up, shredding its pages, but I'm not going to let fear guide me any longer.

If you've opened this book and you're reading my thoughts this very minute, then, really, you're a snoop and a pig but you probably already know that. I'm sure people have told you.

You should know this, too. Everything I've written really happened, exactly like I said. If you don't believe me, that's not my problem.

My immediate problem is Gideon Hawkins.

He's leaving Winterhaven in a few weeks and I hate it. How can he leave me? After all this time, the way I feel about Hawkins is one of the few things I absolutely understand.

I want him with me. Not just as friends. More than friends.

"I've got to do something," he told me, but that just means he needs a direction in his life. If he leaves for Oklahoma Trinity, he'll come back a minister, end up marrying a cute but boring choir singer, and he'll miss out on the best days of his life. The days we should be spending together.

There's still some time before he goes out of state. Time enough, I hope, for me to change things.

Can there be a girlfriend-boyfriend relationship between a soul-deprived monster killer and a preacher's son?

264

Call me crazy (everybody else does) but I think maybe I can make it work....

Chapter Thirty-Three

Before the Beginning, there was the Void. All Creatures
Perverse and Unnatural were imprisoned there.
Before the End, they shall be set free and the Gods of the
Void shall reign again.

– The Book of Forgotten Lies

Their mini-van cresting the hill, Elaine saw a
woman by the roadside. Her hair was cut in short brown
curls and she held a small umbrella over her head.

Hitting the turn lever, her husband began to slow the
car.

"I don't know, Jim," she said. "I don't think this is
such a good idea."

"I swear to God, Lainey, you're getting paranoid in
your old age," Jim told her, the mini-van bumping from
the asphalt and onto the gravel lining. "In the history of
the world, do you think anyone has been mugged by a
middle-aged woman wearing pearls?"

Gravel crunched between the car's wheels as it
rolled to a stop. The woman folded her umbrella and
approached the passenger door.

"I'm so glad you stopped," she told them. "I've been
waiting for ages."

Jim leaned past his wife but not before giving her the look: *See how silly you are.* "Where are you headed?"

"Wenatchee. Apple capital of the world, I'm told."

"We can take you most of the way there. That is, if you don't mind sharing a seat."

"Wonderful." Crossing behind the car, the hitchhiker climbed into the passenger seat. She rested the umbrella beside her as the vehicle returned to the road.

Elaine leaned her arm over the seat. "I'm Elaine, Elaine Koslov. This is my husband, Jim." Concerned, she said, "Is something the matter?"

"Just... just sad, sometimes." The woman wiped at her eyes. "Comes on suddenly." Forcing a smile, she said, "I'm pleased to meet you. I'd appreciate it if you called me Mrs. Jordan."

"Mrs. Jordan?" Jim grinned. "No first name? That's a little old school, isn't it?"

"It's only polite, dear," Mrs. Jordan said. She studied the car seat beside her. "You have a baby."

"Young Master Koslov."

"Sylvester Nathaniel," Elaine said. "I am *not* to be blamed for 'Sylvester'."

"My father's name," Jim explained.

"How old is your son?"

"Tomorrow, he'll be two weeks."

"How adorable," Mrs. Jordan said. She folded her hands atop her lap. "I could simply eat him up."

-end-

267

Author's Note

Several readers have noted similarities between this book, The Atheist's Daughter, *and Stephen King's novel,* Doctor Sleep. *These similarities are only by coincidence.* The Atheist's Daughter *was first published on September 13, 2011.* Doctor Sleep *was published on September 24, 2013.*

About the Authors

"Renée Harrell" is the semi-pseudonym of Renée and Harrell Turner, a wife-and-husband writing team. They have three titles available from *Hunting Monsters Press*: **Something Wicked, The Atheist's Daughter**, and **Aly's Luck.**